VISIONS

VOLUME TWO

....

MILTON J DAVIS

MVmedia, LLC
FAYETTEVILLE GA

MVmedia, LLC
PO Box 143052
Fayetteville, GA 30214

Publisher's Note: This is a work of fiction. Names, characters, places, and incidents are a product of the author's imagination. Locales and public names are sometimes used for atmospheric purposes. Any resemblance to actual people, living or dead, or to businesses, companies, events, institutions, or locales is completely coincidental.

Book Layout ©2017 BookDesignTemplates.com
Cover Art by Jason Reeves
Cover design by Uraeus

Ordering Information:
Quantity sales. Special discounts are available on quantity purchases by corporations, associations, and others. For details, contact the "Special Sales Department" at the address above.

Visions II/Milton J. Davis. -- 1st ed.
ISBN 979-8-9857336-8-6

Contents

To the Visionaries

Manamana

The hammer's rhythm echoed between the oaks, a cadence from a land long lost to its wielder. His skin was black like his ancestors, but the forest in which he and his family lived would be just as alien to them as his baba's homeland would be to him. Yet their blood was the same. This land had taken much from them, but it could not steal his roots.

"Akinbode!"

Akinbode plunged the hot metal into the water before turning to look upon Sally's pleasing umber face. He grinned, matching her mood.

"What is it, labalaba?"

"Supper's ready," she said. "Wash up and come inside."

Sally turned and walked away. Akinbode watched the sway of her wide hips, and his smile grew. For seven years they lived as man and wife, making a good living in the foothills of Shaconage. Trapping was still good, and the woods provided an abundance of game and edible plants. But it was his forging that kept them fed, the nails, tools, knives, and other items he fashioned with his iron, forge, anvil and the secrets from the old world passed on to him from his baba. There were other blacksmiths in the region, but Akinbode's work was the best. For them it was a skill. For Akinbode, it was in his blood.

Sally, Abeni, and Bisi sat at the table, eating their porridge and venison when Akinbode entered. Mobo sat on Sally's lap, eating from his mother's bowl.

"Let you mama eat her own food, boy," Akinbode said.

He grasped Mobo between his calloused hands and lifted him high, making him giggle. Bisi dropped her spoon then raised her arms.

"Me next, baba!"

Akinbode tucked Mobo under his left arm then rubbed Bibi's tousled hair. He sat down before his bowl, picked up his spoon and ate a big scoop of porridge. Mobo reached for the spoon and whined.

"Everything ready for market?" Sally asked.

Akinbode nodded as he fed Mobo.

"How long you expect to be gone?"

"No more than a week if the weather holds up," Akinbode replied. "I should get good trade on the nails. Lots of fixing to be done before the winter blows in."

"Make sure you get seeds," Sally said.

"I will. And pretty dresses for you and the girls."

Sally sucked her teeth. "Don't need no dresses. Just seeds. And maybe some fabric. A little lace would be nice."

Akinbode was about to take another dip into the porridge when Mobo grabbed his spoon. The boy and his sisters giggled as Akinbode made an exaggerated struggle out of it.

"You strong as a bear!"

"You spill that porridge, and you clean it up," Sally said with a grin.

Akinbode sat Mobo down on the floor as he finished his porridge. They were a good family. Living in the wilderness was hard but fair. Nothing was as hard as being owned, and that was something he and Sally struggled to make sure their children would never experience. They both would die before they let that happen. Just like their parents.

After supper Sally prepared the children for bed while Akinbode tended the fire. The girls fell to sleep quickly; Mobo fussed as young ones do when tired until he gave into slumber. Akinbode and Sally joined each other in their loft bed, enjoying the closeness and quiet.

"You don't have to go," Sally said. "We have enough to make it through next market."

"I know," Akinbode replied. "I think the weather will hold off too. But I'm not worried about either of those."

"It's the war," Sally said.

"Yes."

Akinbode pulled Sally closer, smiling as she pressed her bottom against his groin.

"Who do you think will win?" she asked.

"Doesn't matter," Akinbode replied. "Things will be the same for folks like us."

"They say the redcoats are offering freedom for negroes that fight for the crown."

"Who told you that?"

"Martha," Sally said. "She heard it at the fort."

"We're already free," Akinbode said.

"As long as we live here."

Akinbode rose on his elbow.

"You don't like it here?" he asked.

Sally shrugged.

"I like it well enough," she replied. "But it would be nice to travel without fear of slave hunters. I hope the Crown wins."

"If we stay where we are, it won't matter," Akinbode said.

Akinbode laid down and pulled Sally closer.

"No more talk about rebels or redcoats. I'll be gone for a week. Let's take advantage of this quiet time."

Sally reached back, placing her hand between his legs.

* * *

Akinbode woke the next day before dawn. He eased out of the bed so not to wake Sally, then felt his way through the dark to his chest. Opening it slowly, he reached inside, touching about until he felt the cold glass of his drinking spirits.

Akinbode carried the bottle outside with him to where his parents were buried. He knelt before them then closed his eyes as he poured out a portion of the alcoholic brew.

"Baba, mama. Thank you for your love and your wisdom. Please watch over Sally and the children as I make this journey, and please walk with me for protection."

Sally was awake when he returned to house. She helped him dress, then the two of them went to the stables to load the horse and mules. Once everything was secure, they shared a long kiss.

"Be careful my husband," Sally said.

"I will, my wife. Kiss the children for me."

Akinbode set out for the market with the sunrise. The journey took him the entire day, the sight and smells of the gathering reaching him at dusk. He decided to spend the night in the forest because it had been a long time since he'd been to such a large gathering. He enjoyed being in the wilderness with his family and large gatherings often led to discord. After securing his horse and mule, he unpacked his most valuable items, using a bundle as a head rest for the night. Sleep came quickly, the emptiness replaced by memories of mama and baba. At least these were pleasant ones. He remembered baba pouring libations to the ancestors and giving grains and meat to Oshun before heating his forge and adding the secret blend of metals and nyama that gave his iron strength and flexibility unlike any other. He remembered working in the fields with mama, slinging clay balls at the birds attempting to steal their grain and helping her churn butter. Those memories faded into mist as he opened his eyes to the bright morning chill.

The market was in full swing by the time Akinbode arrived. He nodded his way through the crowd of trappers, hunters, farmers and merchants, finally finding a clear spot at the edge of the crowd. There was a line of people behind him, eager for his wares. Akinbode opened his mule's pack, taking out the thick blanket Sally had woven for him. As he spread the blanket, he heard someone clear his throat. He turned then smiled.

"Kana'ti," he said.

"O'siyo, oganalii," Kana'ti replied.

They hugged, pounding each other's back with their fists.

"I wasn't sure I'd see you," Akinbode said. "I heard your clan had migrated west."

"The white men kill all the beaver," Kana'ti replied. "We go where we can live. But I had to come back to see you, and trade for your iron."

"What do you have?" Akinbode asked.

Kana'ti opened the pouch hanging from his waste. Akinbode reached into the bag and took out one of the brown stones. It was iron ore, the purest Akinbode had seen in some time.

"I think we can do some business," he said to his friend. He ambled to his horse, continuing to unpack.

Akinbode noticed three men approaching from the corner of his eye. They weren't from the valley; he knew everyone who lived there. One of them wore the uniform of the rebels. He continued to unpack his horse as they came closer.

"Boy," the younger man said. "Are you Akinbode?

Akinbode whispered a curse before turning about.

"I don't see any boys standing around here, stranger."

"I beg your pardon," the man in the uniform said. "Are you Akinbode?"

"I am."

"My name is Captain Henry Parker," the man said, his hand extended. Akinbode looked at his hand then continued unpacking.

"Whose captain?" he asked. "I don't see no Redcoats here."

Captain Parker frowned. "I represent the Continental Army. And we need your assistance."

"So y'all calling yourselves a real army?" Akinbode asked. "What y'all need from me?"

"The people in these parts say you're the finest blacksmith in the colonies," the captain replied, ignoring Akinbode's insult. "Our army needs men like you to help our cause."

"I'm not a part of your cause," Akinbode said.

The young man stepped up, a sneer on his face. Akinbode noticed a wisp of a moustache on his upper lip.

"We're fighting for our freedom, our liberty!" he said.

"Your freedom," Akinbode said. "I suspect when all this is said and done my people will still be slaves."

The young man looked away, embarrassed. The captain cleared his throat.

"There's always the possibility . . ."

"I'm not interested in possibilities," Akinbode said. "And I'm not interested in your war. Besides, the redcoats are offering freedom and land to those that fight for them."

"The captain and his men said nothing. Akinbode grinned.

"Now if y'all will excuse me, I got merchandise to trade before nightfall."

"We can make you!" the young man blurted. "Story is your daddy was a runaway. That makes you property of whoever owned him."

Akinbode picked up his musket. He faced the three men with it cradled in his arms.

"You see this?" he said. "My baba named it Manamana. That means lightning in the old tongue. You probably heard of it."

The trio exchanged nervous glances.

He patted the stock. "You see these beads in the stock? Each one represents a man who tried to make me property. You ready to join them?"

The younger man turned red.

"Captain, are you going to let this nig . . ."

The captain raised his hand, quieting the man.

"Don't be stupid, Taylor. Look around you."

Taylor turned his head. A crowd had gathered, a mixed group of native people and colonists. None of their expressions were happy, and all held their muskets at the ready.

Akinbode grinned.

"I think it's time you took your leave, captain," he said. "And if I were you, I'd never come back."

The captain tipped his hat.

"We'll talk again," he said. "That I assure you."

The captain and his soldiers backed away, their muskets ready. Akinbode watched them melding into the surroundings then continued to unpack his horse.

We should go after them," Kana'ti said. "Kill them and take their scalps to the British fort. They might give us a reward."

"Don't want to have anything to do with the redcoats or the rebels," Akinbode said. "They'll clear out if they know what's good for them. That captain seems to have some common sense."

"I don't know," Kana'ti said.

"Look, you want to trade or what?" Akinbode asked.

The day rushed by like water in a swollen river. The nails were in demand, and Akinbode was able to haggle a good trade for the items Sally requested. By nightfall he was tired and satisfied. He could stay another day and enjoy the company of friends, but the visit by the colonials made him nervous despite his word with Kana'ti. It was better for him to head out at first light, putting as much distance between him and the market possible.

Akinbode woke to another chilly morning. After a quick meal of dried meat, he was on his way back. He considered taking the western trail along the river, but then decided to take the southwest route. The trail was rugged, but his pack animals were familiar with it, and the terrain would slow down anyone attempting to follow. He traveled until noon then rested under the branches of a poplar stand atop a steep hill overlooking a narrow stream. As his animals grazed on the undergrowth, he looked down at the waterway, still swollen from the winter runoff. The quietness soothed him, and his thoughts drifted to Sally and the children. The wilderness was unforgiving, but if you respected it, there was much peace to be had. Their lives were much better than his parents', and he would do whatever it took to keep it so.

Akinbode spotted movement near the stream bank and his complacency faded. The rebels from the market crept into view, walking in single file with their muskets held at the ready. They were searching for him. If he stayed still, they would continue down the river and never notice him. But following the stream trail would eventually lead to his homestead. There was the possibility they would turn back, but Akinbode couldn't leave it to chance. He stood then walked to his horse, taking Mamamana from its leather sheath, then securing his knives around his waist. He walked back to the hill's edge. The troops had halted and were setting up camp. While the others worked on the camp, two soldiers faded into the woods. Akinbode slung the musket over his shoulder then proceeded down the hill into the dense brush while listening for the scouts sent to find him.

It didn't take long for him to locate both men. The thick forest forced them to stay close to each other as they searched for him. As much as Akinbode wanted to use Manamana, the proximity to the others wouldn't allow it. He would have to get closer.

The trees thinned as the interlopers climbed the hill. The men separated, and Akinbode chose his first target. Working his way ahead of them, he found a clearing that would put him in the path of the first warrior. He lay on his back, in the middle of the path, then waited. The ground vibrations transformed into soft footfalls. Akinbode remained still.

"Benjamin!" the man shouted. "I found him! Looks like he's dead."

Akinbode sprang upright, driving his knife into the man's gut as he pulled him down. He plunged the knife into his throat before he could cry out then pulled the dying man into the bushes.

"Michael!" the other man called.

Akinbode decided to leave Michael's body in the path. He slipped into the underbrush and waited for Benjamin. The man ran up the path, his musket lowered. He stumbled to a stop when he saw his companion's body.

"Michael!"

Akinbode sprang from hiding, knife in his left hand, tomahawk in his right. Benjamin pivoted toward him, trying to level the musket. Akinbode knocked the rifle aside with his knife then chopped Benjamin's neck with his tomahawk. Benjamin screamed and his hand tensed. The musket fired, sound and smoke disorienting Akinbode for a moment. He pounced on the man again, driving his knife into his gut three times before fleeing back into the bush.

Akinbode would normally linger to make sure his opponent was dead, but he knew the musket's report would bring the others. He plunged back into the undergrowth, heading for higher ground. As he weaved through the thicket, he heard the rebels working their way toward their fallen comrades. A slight grin came to his face; unlike the ones that attacked him, these men were hunters, doing their best to move silently through unfamiliar ground.

He reached his perch then looked down at the scene. The soldiers converged on the body, the captain the last man to emerge from the brush. He examined the bodies as the others scanned the surroundings. Akinbode raised Manamana, taking aim at the leader. One shot could end this pursuit, or maybe it would bring more soldiers seeking him and his family. He lowered his weapon. The captain spoke, and the others melded into the brush. They were not breaking off their pursuit.

"So be it," Akinbode whispered.

Akinbode was standing when someone fell on him, pushing him back into the dirt. A rope brushed his neck and he jammed his hand between it and his throat as his assailant attempted to pull tight. Throwing his left elbow backwards, he struck the person as he rolled, pitching them off his back.

The only reason he was alive was that they wanted to capture him. He jumped to his feet in a crouch, knife and tomahawk at the ready, staring into the angry face of the young soldier who had insulted him earlier.

"I don't care what the captain said," the man hissed. "I'm killing your nigger ass!"

The men lunged. Akinbode blocked the man's thrust with his tomahawk then swept his feet, slashing his arm before he hit the ground. He swung his tomahawk down, but the revolutionist rolled and his blade struck dirt. The man was quick like a mountain cat, springing to his feet and swinging out with his hatchet to keep Akinbode at bay.

"I found him!" he shouted. Akinbode feinted high with his blades and the revolutionist's arms rose to block the fake attack. He kicked the rebel hard in the stomach and he doubled over and fell to the ground, his head crashing into the dirt. Akinbode ran. He wanted to finish the man, but the others were coming. He was cresting the hill when a volley of musket fire shattered the quiet. A musket ball slammed his right shoulder, and he stumbled forward. Gritting his teeth against the pain, he kept running.

Akinbode reached the crest of the hill then sprinted down the slope toward the creek. Crossing the swollen waterway would make him an easy target, but he had no intention of doing so. He crouched, running parallel to the bank until he found what he was seeking.

The cave entrance was barely visible. Akinbode found it years ago by chance while tracking a wounded beaver. Many times since then it had served him, mainly a place to hide provisions or furs. This time, he hoped it would save his life.

He splashed into the creek, wading for a moment then exiting the frigid waters and falling to his hands and knees. His shoulder ached as he crawled into the hollowed hideout. Luckily it was empty. Akinbode twisted about so he faced the entrance, Manamana loaded and primed. He placed the metal musket beside him as he felt for the wound in darkness. It wasn't as bad as he feared, but he would have to treat it soon before it became infected. His situation was desperate; if the soldiers discovered the cave, he'd have no way out. His only hope would be that they still thought him valuable. If not, this hole would be his grave.

Akinbode heard splashing and picked up Manamana.

"You sure you saw him go this way?"

"Yes, sir."

"Look for signs on the opposite bank. He couldn't have gone far. I'm sure I shot him."

The splashing stopped before the cave entrance. Akinbode saw a pair of boots blocking the entrance. The revolutionists continue to talk as they searched for him. The boots shifted.

"What a minute. What's this?"

A barrage of musket fire echoed into the cave. The boots before the cave disappeared. Akinbode grinned as he heard familiar whoops and cries and more musket fire. He waited until the shooting and voices faded before crawling out of his hideout. A body lay on the bank in front of the cave, the remains of one of the revolutionists.

"I see your hiding hold served you well again."

Akinbode turned his head. Kana'ti sat on the ground, his musket laying across his knees. The Cherokee warrior chewed on a blade of grass.

"You followed me?"

"Yes. I knew they would follow you, just like you did. The whites are relentless."

Kana'ti stood and ambled down the hill to him. A frown came to his face.

"You're shot."

Akinbode nodded then turned to show his wound.

"Let's get you home them," Kana'ti said.

Akinbode followed his friend up the hill. As they reached the hilltop, the others had gathered. It was a collection of his friends.

"You'll have to move," Kana'ti said. "Go to the British. They want the same thing from you, but they'll pay you for it."

Akinbode shook his head. "White men are the same, no matter what color they wear. I'll go back to my family and travel west."

Kana'ti's face became solemn.

"They will eventually come."

"That's true," Akinbode agreed. "But for now, it's the only choice we have."

Kana'ti nodded.

"Come brother. Let's get that wound treated and get you home. Sally would never forgive me if you died."

"Me, either."

They laughed as they joined the others and walked back to the market. Kana'ti took him the local healer, Immokalee, who cleaned his wound then sewed it shut.

"You must rest," the woman advised. "Give the stitching time to set.

Akinbode shook his head. "I have to return home now. There may be more men looking for me."

"We will go with you," Kana' ti said.

"I don't . . ."

"Yes you do," Kana'ti finished.

Akinbode hated to admit he was wrong, but he was.

"Let's go then."

The party took the main road. They rode hard, hoping to make it to his cabin before darkness. They were nearing the cabin when the air crackled with musket fire.

"No!" Akinbode shouted. He spurred his horse into a full gallop, flinching with each shot fire. Though he shook with anger, he knew not to ride into the clearing. Whoever was attacking his family would use cover.

Kana'ti and the others caught up to him and they rushed to the cabin. To Akinbode's relief, the shooting ceased.

"We don't wish to harm you," a rumbling voice called out. "Throw your weapon outside and surrender. You will be freed once we have Akinbode."

Sally would know what the man said was a lie. They would be taken back to the colony and sold.

Kana'ti crawled to his side.

"I see eight, no more than ten," Kana'ti whispered.

Akinbode nodded.

"Each warrior pick a man then wait for my signal."

Kana'ti nodded then crawled away.

Akinbode found his target, a tall wide man wearing a coonskin cap. Probably a mountain man that decided to take sides. He loaded Manamana then drew a bead on the man's head.

The bobwhite whistle let Akinbode know everyone was in place. He took a deep breath, then whistled back.

Musket fire roared like a thunderclap. The rebels fell simultaneously and Akinbode rose to his feet before the gunsmoke cleared. He sprinted across the expanse, hopping over the body of the dead trapper. The cabin door swung open and Sally emerged, holding her musket. A relieved smile came to her face as she recognized Akinbode and they ran to each other. They dropped their weapons and hugged.

"I knew you would come," she said.

"I shouldn't have left," he replied.

"Baba!"

The children spilled from the cabin then formed a hug around their legs. Akinbode peered over his shoulder; Kana'ti and his warriors searched the rebels' bodies for valuables, shot and powder.

He looked into Sally's watery eyes.

"I guess I should have stayed home."

Sally squeezed him. "You're home now."

Kana'ti sauntered up to them.

"We should go," he said.

Akinbode gazed at their cabin and the land they'd worked so hard. His eyes ended at the ancestor tree where his parents were buried. Home meant many things, but home was truly where he and his family thrived.

"Sally?"

She squeezed his hand.

"It's time," she said.

Akinbode, Sally and the children went to the cabin to gather what they could carry. By nightfall, they were gone.

The Killing Storms
(A Ki Khanga Adventure)

Kwanele kaDumisani was a rich man. His umuzi was one of the most successful in Zambululand and the largest of his city. His herds were enormous, the patterned bovines swarming the hillsides in the thousands. Others of such wealth would claim the title of inkosi and rule over the region, but Kwanele was a modest and humble man. He spent his time discussing the business of the day and other eso- teric matters with his neighbors while tending his herds with his sons and grandsons. Sharing wisdom was status enough for him; Kwanele had no desire to lead or command.

The day began as normal, following a routine that had existed long before Kwanele emerged into this world from his mama's womb. After breakfast with his family, he meandered among his herd as he waited for the bachelors from the surrounding umuzis to join him. There he remained, tending to his bovine wealth and sharing his wisdom with the young men hoping to one day be as well-known as him.

The sun was near the end of its journey across the sky, eagerly descending to its resting place be- yond the hills. As he watched the shadows run down the steep slopes, Kwanele noticed a dark shape rise above the distant peaks. He strained his eyes to make it out and was disturbed.

Kwanele trotted up to his eldest son who stood nearby watching their cattle.

"Mandla."

"Yes, baba?"

"Look to the hills and tell me what you see."

Mandla turned to the peaks.

"I see . . . a cloud?"

"I do, too."

"But it is not rainy season. Why would there be clouds, baba?"

"Not only that, but they also approach from the wrong direction."

Son and father eyes met.

"Run ahead," Kwanele said. "Tell you mothers and siblings to stay inside their homes."

"What are you going to do?" Mandla asked.

"Summon Sibongakone. Maybe the old ngona knows."

Mandla ran to the outer ring of the umuzi. Kwanele hated leaving his herd unattended, but this was an important matter. Rain during the dry season meant unexpected flooding which could cause much damage to his umuzis and others. He was almost to his thorn fence when a cold wind pushed against him, causing him to shiver. He looked to the mountains again; the clouds were much closer, the dark canopy churning like a swollen river. There was no way he would make it to Sibongakone's umuzi before the rain. He turned back to gather his herd and drive them to the interior pen.

Lightning flased in the clouds, and thunder shook the ground beneath his feet. The startled herd answered with frightened bellows. Kwanele picked up his pace, fear in his eyes. The last thing he needed was a stampede. He worked his way among them, patting their necks and heads as he hummed. It seemed to be working when the second round of thunder began. The herd bolted in every direction, cows, calves and bulls fleeing the coming maelstrom. Kwanele ran to his great wife's home, deftly dodging the terrified beasts. He was almost there when lightning struck the thatch roof, igniting it. The door flew open, and his family spilled out, eyes wide with terror. The lightning struck again and again, hitting each of his homes and setting them ablaze. As his family huddled around him under the black sky, Kwanele realized that despite the wind, clouds and lightning, there was no rain. A shrill cry ripped the air, bringing his hands to his ears and his eyes to the sky. Something moved within the clouds, a shape that seemed familiar yet too massive to be true. He was attempting to understand when lightning enveloped him, sending him into eternal darkness.

*　*　*

The royal ibuthu set out for Inanga two weeks after hearing of the deadly storm. The slow pace to the village frustrated the warriors, but they had no choice in the matter. The inkosi insisted his sonchai, Thulani, accompany them, and the middle-aged man was not used to the rigors of the march. He complained at every opportunity, stopping frequently to rub his sore feet or stretch his back.

Thulani took an ointment from his medicine bag. He dipped two fingers into the gourd then spread the concoction onto his calloused palms before rubbing his aching feet. The others stood nearby glaring at him, but he didn't care. These were his feet and they needed attention.

"Are you done?" Nkosenye asked. The towering induna was the leader of the ibuthu, and while he commanded the warriors, he had no authority over Thulani.

"When I stand and begin walking, you'll know I'm done," Thulani replied. It helped that he had a deep commanding voice that conveyed his spiritual powers. Still, Nkosenye seemed unaffected. He approached Thulani, a mean frown on his rugged face.

"Maybe I should carry you, like the baby you are," Nkosenye said.

Thulani's foot pain subsided, and he smiled.

"Maybe you should, but not today. Our destination is only a few strides away over the next hill."

"How do you know this?" Nkosenye asked.

"Because I am a sonchai."

Thulani stood then faced Nkosenye. The inkosi's sonchai was not a small man. He matched Nkosenye in height and girth, although his body was not muscled like the warrior's. Combined with his powerful ashé, he was not a man easily intimidated. Nkosenye stepped aside as Thulani made his way toward the hill. Nkosenye signaled the others and they followed. As they reached the crest their destination came into view. Thulani was about to speak when a sudden pain struck him in the gut like a war club. He fell to his knees.

"What is it now?" Nkosenye said without sympathy. "Are you hungry?"

"Go ahead," Thulani replied. "I will be down soon."

Nkosenye and the others descended the hill. Thulani sat back on his haunches, looking in the distance at the ravaged umuzi as he massaged his stomach. He could sense from a distance that this had been an ordinary storm, yet his skills were not needed there. His pain came from a different source, one which he had to visit by himself to ascertain what had occurred in the village. He waited until the ibuthu was crossing the stream separating the hill from the umuzi's mound before struggling to his feet and heading east toward the source of his discomfort and possibly the origin of the umuzi's demise.

-2-

Izegbe perched proudly on her war bull, swaying with its laconic pace. The sun's warmth rested gently on her shoulders and those of her entourage, its light dimmed sporadically by clouds. The celebration drummers walked in double lines before her, their large drums strapped to their backs. They sang, their melodic voices adding to the levity of the journey. She looked to her left at Enomwoyi and chuckled. The woman was barely on her bull, riding fast asleep. Her servants would catch her if she leaned too far, pushing her back upright.

"Hey!" Izegbe shouted.

Enomwoyi jumped and instinctively reached for her sword. Izegbe and the others laughed. Enomwoyi was not amused. She glared at her servants who looked away.

"You think this is funny?" she shouted. "I should chop off your heads!"

"You should stay awake, that's what you should do," Izegbe said.

Enomwoyi jerked her head toward Izegbe.

"This is your fault," she said. "I wouldn't be embarrassing myself if not for this boring journey."

"I didn't ask you to come," Izegbe replied. "You volunteered. This is my home, not yours."

"A Mino never travels alone," Enomwoyi said. "Especially one of the Ngola's Petals."

"I wouldn't have been alone. I have my servants and my drummers. Most of all, I have Gbeganganno."

The sacred shield bounced off Izegbe's back. It had been forged at the beginning of time, at least that's what the geles said. The intricate face which filled the shield's center was that of Noxolo Ode, first Ngola of Matamba. Gbeganganno was imbued with its special powers by Owo, as were all the weapons of the Petals. They were the talisman of the first Mino, preserved over the centuries and passed on to those warriors that possessed the high skills and the ashé required to wield them.

"Still, we Mino do not walk alone," Enomwoyi said.

Their banter was interrupted by the return of the hunters. The men had been hired to find the road to Izegbe's village, Nati. Izegbe left her home as a child to serve the Ngola and did not remember the way. The winded men smiled, their traditional brown cotton shirts and pants soaked with sweat.

"We have found the village," the elder warrior said.

"Good, Boubacar," Izegbe replied. "Did you inform the village elders of our arrival?"

"Yes, aunt. They are very excited. They summoned your mama and baba. They could not stop crying when they heard it was you."

Izegbe's eyes glistened. She was joyous knowing that both of her parents still lived. She was a girl when the Ngola's recruiters came to her village seeking girls to replenish the Mino ranks. The war against Asanteman was victorious yet costly, and new warriors were needed. It was every girls' dream to be selected and a high honor for her family. It was also a blessing, for the Ngola paid a handsome lobola to the family of those who were chosen. It was twenty seasons ago when she left; she had not been back since.

"How far are we away?" she asked Boubacar.

Boubacar looked at his fellow hunter.

Only a few hundred strides," the younger man said. "We should be reaching the farms soon."

"Drummers!" Izegbe shouted. "Time to announce our arrival!"

Ehizoke, the lead drummer, raised her sticks in response. The other players removed the instruments from their backs then balanced them on their heads.

"Aya!" Ehizoke shouted.

"Aye!" the drummers responded.

The cadence they played was a new one the Ngola commissioned just for Izegbe's homecoming. Enomwoyi's eyes lit up and a smile broke on her face like sunrise.

"Now this is a homecoming!"

Izegbe sang and the others quickly joined in.

Wake up mama!
Wake up baba!
Your baby has come home,
Your baby has come home!

Wake up aunt!
Wake up uncle!
Your niece has come home,
Your niece has come home.

Wake up village!
Wake up land!

A warrior returns,
And she is not alone!

The people had gathered by the time they reached the farms, lining the village road and straining their necks to see their daughter return. They waved and cheered, some of them singing along and following the procession to the village center. Izegbe stopped singing, allowing her servants and the drummers to herald her return.

They arrived at the village center to find the elders sitting under the canopy of the meeting tree. Izegbe's dignity broke down when she saw her mama and baba sitting with the elders. They were older and stouter, but their joyful faces were the same as they were when she left the village almost twenty seasons ago. She jumped from her war bull and ran to them, arms wide and cheeks wet from her tears.

"Mama! Baba!"

Asoro and Nanare jumped to their feet, running as fast as their aged limbs allowed. Parents and daughter met and fell to their knees in hugs and kisses. Other family members gathered around them, singing and giving praises to Oyo. When Izegbe finally stood she hugged and kissed them as well. Once the greetings had settled and the music ceased, Omosupe, the village chief, stood and opened her arms.

"Welcome home, Izegbe," Omosupe said. "We have missed our daughter."

Izegbe embraced the chief. "And I have missed you."

Omosupe stepped away and regarded her.

"You have done well," she said. "The Ngola has honored you."

"Yes, she has," Izegbe confirmed. "I have done my best to make you all proud of me. The name of our village is spoken with pride."

"We know your journey has been long. We will let you spend time with your family. Tonight, we will celebrate your return."

"Thank you, Aunt Omosupe," Izegbe said. "It is wonderful to be home."

The chief raised her hand and the drumming resumed. Izegbe danced with her village, her servants and her family. The light dimmed and she looked into the sky. Clouds gathered over them, an unusual sight for this time of year. But she would not let rain dampen her mood. She was home. She would make the best of it.

The clouds increased as Izegbe and her family made their way to the family compound. By the time they reached their destination, the sky looked ominous.

"This is odd," mama said. "Rainy season is weeks away."

"Oyo blesses us," baba replied. "An early rain means a fertile season."

Lightning flashed and everyone jumped. The thunder followed, a sound that shook the nearby building. Izegbe's smile faded as the Voice stirred on her back. She looked at Enomwoyi. Pillar, her spear, glowed green. Enomwoyi's face reflected her concern.

"This is not normal," she said.

"Everyone get inside now!" Izegbe shouted.

Villagers scattered in every direction. Mama tugged at Izegbe's sleeve.

"What is happening?" she asked.

"I don't know," Izegbe answered. "But it is not good."

No sooner did she speak those last words was she blinded by light and pain.

-3-

Thulani knew he was near the sonchai's lair when he spotted the protection talisman in the trees. Mutilated bodies of monkeys and birds hung from the branches smelling of death and other repulsive odors. The visible warnings were meant to keep the timid away. The sonchai reached out with his ashé and felt the more dangerous talisman, those that would harm anyone that did not heed those displayed. He was impressed; this sonchai was skilled. He continued, confident that his grisgris was more than adequate in protecting him from these deterrents.

As neared the sonchai's den, he couldn't help but notice that the defenses had not been maintained for some time. The evidence lent more strength to what he suspected, but he would not be sure until he found the sonchai's hut. He knew he was close when the emanations from the talisman decreased. Soon after the woods cleared, revealing a large home surrounded by a field of unkempt herbs. Most of the plants were familiar to Thulani, yet some of them were strange. The stench of death invaded his nostrils as he neared the hut. He knew what he would find before he pushed the door aside. The sonchai's body lay on the dirt floor, his right hand clutching a large, long necked gourd. By the looks of him he had been dead for at least a week, probably more. Gourds and cups of various sizes sat on the table before the sonchai's body.

"What were you up to, brother?" Thulani whispered.

He went to the table for a closer look at the calabashes. Thulani opened them all, smelling and tasting their contents. With each inspection the purpose of the ingredients painted a clearer image. When Thulani tasted the last ingredient, he knew what the dead sonchai had done. He knelt beside dead sorcerer's body then pried the gourd from his hand. He shook the container before opening it. He sniffed it and the aroma confirmed his suspicions.

Thulani tied the gourd to his waist belt. He turned the sonchai onto his stomach then studied what was left of his back. Six jagged wounds ran from his shoulders to his waist.

"At least you tried to fight," Thulani said.

He searched the hut but found nothing else of importance. Thulani left the hut then walked behind it. He discovered a small cage hanging from an acacia tree's limb. Thulani opened the cage; there were bird droppings and feathers on the bottom. He took an empty pouch from his gris-gris bag and filled it with the waste. He wasn't sure if he would need it later, but he would rather have it and not need it than not to have it all.

There was one more thing to do. Thulani gathered small branches then stacked them against the sonchai's hut. He took out his sparking stone and set the branches afire; a few moments later the house was consumed in flames.

"May the ancestors welcome you at the meeting tree," Thulani said.

Having found what he was looking for and performing his duty, Thulani made his way back to the warriors and the village.

* * *

The umuzis were under repair when Thulani returned. Instead of seeking Nkosenye and the others he asked about until he learned of the healers' whereabouts. A small village like this usually had one sangoma and inyanga; in some cases, one person performed both duties. Her name was Sibongile. Thulani came upon her caring for an elderly woman outside her hut. She was young, the initiation scars on her cheeks recent. The healer turned as he approached, a frown marring her pleasant face.

"*Sawubona*," he said.

"What do you want, sonchai?" Sibongile replied.

"How are the people?" he said.

"They are as well as they can be, considering they were attacked by a storm."

Thulani stood beside Sibongile, studying the elderly woman.

"Her arm is broken," he said.

"What do you know of healing?" Sibongile asked. "You are a sonchai. You cause harm. You don't prevent it."

"I have other skills," Thulani replied.

"Deadly skills," Sibongile said. "It's the only reason the inkosi would want you."

Sibongile was trying his patience.

"Did anyone speak of seeing anything else beside the storm?" he asked.

"No," Sibongile replied.

"That is not true," Sibongile's elderly patient said.

"What is your name, aunt?" Thulani asked.

"Owethu."

"What did they see?"

Owethu grimaced as Sibongile set her arm.

"When the winds swirled on the ground, many said they saw a creature within."

"Did they say what it looked like?"

Owethu began to lift her arms, but Sibongile shook her head.

"They say it was like a large bird."

Sibongile looked at Thulani, a worried expression on her face. She knows, Thulani thought.

"Thank you, aunt."

Thulani hurried away to find Nkosenye. The gruff induna supervised the rebuilding of the chief's compound. He stood with his hands clasped behind his back, shouting orders to his warriors and the other men of the village.

"Nkosenye!" Thulani called. The induna turned and frowned.

"So, you have returned," he said. "How disappointing. I assume you did not come back to help us rebuild. I'm sure your feet would disagree."

"I have no problem with building homes," Thulani replied. "But more important matters call for my attention."

"What could be more important?"

"I think I know what caused this."

Nkosenye rolled his eyes.

"It was a storm."

Thulani shook his head. "I wish it was that simple."

"What are you talking about, sonchai?"

Thulani walked away.

"When you return to the inkosi tell him I am looking for something important. Tell him that if I find it, he will be the most powerful man in Zambululand."

And so will I, Thulani mused.

"He already is!" Nkosenye called out.

"Not like this," Thulani replied. "Nothing like this."

-4-

Izegbe returned to the living in pieces. The screaming startled her from unconsciousness; she regained her sight moments later. She stood then staggered, the storm raging overhead. Despite its fury, no rain fell. Izegbe looked down and found her shield and sword. She picked up her weapons. Though it was a storm, she sensed she would need them.

"Enomwoyi!" she shouted.

"I'm here!" her sister shouted back.

Izegbe turned her head and found her sister rising from the ground, her spear still gripped in her hand. She joined her and together they took stock of the situation. Homes burned around them; villagers sprawled in the streets. Some of the bodies were the drummers that had come with them. Some moved; others didn't. Those still alive and conscious ran about in panic, seeking shelter wherever they could find it. The lightning flashed, but this was no random pattern. Every bolt hit a home or a person. The clouds descended lower with every second until they hovered just over head.

"Look!" Enomwoyi shouted as she pointed with her spear.

A pair of bird-like claws emerged from the clouds before them. A creature like nothing Izgebe had ever seen appeared, a large bird resembling the vultures of the High Valley. White feathers covered its body, the plumage luminescent like lightning. The bird creature raised its head then let out a cry that penetrated Izegbe's ears, making her wince. It hopped to the nearest body then pecked it with its sharp beak. Blood flowed from the person's neck. The creature bent closer then lapped the blood from the wound with a hummingbird-like tongue.

"No!" Enomwoyi shouted. Her spear glowed as she threw it, streaking toward the creature faster than any normal spear should. It was almost to the creature when it jerked its head about. Its eyes flashed and lightning blew the spear aside. Izegbe grabbed Enomwoyi by her shirt then dragged her close as she raised her shield. The bolts meant for her missed.

"Noxolo!" she yelled. Izegbe felt the shield shift. Though she could not see it, she knew Noxolo had come. The eyes of the shield face were open, as well as the mouth. When the bird creature sent its bolts toward them again, the shield howled, the sound blast deflecting the attack. Izegbe peeked around her shield. The creature had abandoned its victims and focused on them. The bird cried out then bombarded the shield with lightning.

"Oyo protect us," Izegbe whispered as the shield shook with each strike.

"If I could get my spear, I can kill this thing," Enomwoyi said.

"No," Izegbe replied. "If you step from behind Noxolo, it will kill you. We will move forward until we are close enough to attack. Are you ready?"

"Yes," Enomwoyi replied.

They stepped in unison as they were trained. The bird thing continued to bombard them with bolts, the thunder deafening. Though Izegbe feared for her life, she was grateful that the creature's attention was on them and not the hapless villagers. With their weapons and skills, they had a better chance to survive.

"To the left!" Enomwoyi shouted.

Izegbe looked to her left. Enomwoyi spear lay on the ground, which meant they were close to the creature. They shuffled to the weapon and Enomwoyi smiled as she picked it up.

"Now we can kill this thing," Enomwoyi said.

The bird thing cried out as if responding to Enomwoyi challenge. The lighting barrage ceased. Izegbe looked over her shield; the bird thing was gone. She lowered her shield then looked about. The bird shrieked again, its voice coming from above. The warriors looked up together. The bird creature loomed over them, its eyes burning like white fire.

"Time to die!" Enomwoyi shouted. As she drew back to throw, the bird thing released its fury. This time Izegbe was not fast enough. The bolts struck them both, blasting them far apart. Izegbe lay stunned for a moment, then scrambled to her feet to find her sister. Enomwoyi jerked on her back while lightning struck her again and again. Izegbe rushed to her, flinging herself between the creature and Enomwoyi body. The lightning attack ceased, replaced by torrential rain. Izegbe struggled to her feet then stumbled to Enomwoyi spear. She lifted it then searched the sky but was blinded by the downpour. Frustrated, she tossed the spear away then went to her sister's side. Enomwoyi lay motionless, her eyes wide despite the rain. It took Izegbe a moment before she realized Enomwoyi was dead. She closed her sister's eyes then lay beside her, crying into her chest. The rain lessened, the clouds thinning then departing. Izegbe sat upright then gazed upon the devastation. Her home village burned. So many lay dead or dying as the sun appeared through the remaining clouds. She looked at her sister again.

"I'm so sorry," she said. "You should not have come."

Izegbe stood then lurched toward the others emerging from hiding. She would help heal the living, then help bury the dead. Once that was complete, she would find the creature that took her friend's life and destroyed her village. Once she found it, she would kill it.

-5-

Thulani chewed a kola nut as he gazed upon the Umese River from atop the steep hill. The wide laconic waterway served as the border between Zambuluand and Matamba; to cross it would put his life in danger. There was no love lost between the two countries. The hate was so deep that both used the other as the forge that molded their warriors. He raised his gourd containing the impundulu gris-gris and frowned at it glowed. The creature had definitely crossed the river, probably to wreak havoc on the unsuspecting Matambans. The inkosi would be pleased; to know the creature was killing his enemies would make him smile. But Thulani knew the value of it. Such power shouldn't be wasted in random carnage. It should be trained and focused like the weapon it was.

He shrugged, took his axe from his waist belt then sauntered down the hill to the river's edge. He built a raft from surrounding saplings, tying the narrow trees together with bark strips. It was an adequate effort, sturdy enough to get him across the river, or so he hoped. Thulani located another sapling and fashion a pole from it, of which he used to push himself across the river. Once on the other side he hid the raft inside a clump of thorn bushes just in case he returned the same way.

Thulani walked the remaining day, using the gourd as a guide and avoiding inhabited areas. At dusk he found a place to sleep, feasting on dried meat and sorghum from his provisions. He slept fitfully, waking throughout the night to shake the gris-gris gourd to make sure he was heading in the right direction. The contents continued to glow. He was traveling deeper into Matamba, which did not bode well. If he was lucky, he would find the impundulu and subdue it before he was discovered. If he wasn't, fisi would feast on his bones.

One week into his search the gourd contents began sputtering. The impundulu was near. He slowed his pace, scrutinizing his surroundings with his ashé in search of spiritual spoor. Half a day into his hunt he saw the signs of a nearby village. Thulani frowned, knowing what he would find when he reached it. He decided to set up camp for the rest of the day and continue to the village that night, if any of it remained.

Darkness fell over the land like a heavy blanket. Thulani woke and gathered his things before searching for the village. He came upon it a few hours later. The glow from the huts relieved him; the impundulu had descended on the village, but some of the villagers survived. He would wait until the fires died before entering the village for more gris-gris to continue his search.

The village firelight faded away and Thulani crept to the town. The sounds of sleeping villagers mingled with the rustling of farm animals, disguising his movements. A queasy feeling emerged filled his gut; he was near the area where the impundulu struck. The ruined huts were near the center of the village, wood and other objects still scattered about. Thulani closed his eyes, reaching out with his ashé. A scene coalesced in his mind; a terrible image of the village being attacked. Lightning flashed, striking homes and people at random. Then he saw it, the image of the impundulu descending from the storm clouds to feast on the blood of its victims. But something stopped it. He shifted his spectral view to two warriors, one with an enchanted spear, the other carrying a shield holding a formidable spirit.

"Mino," he whispered. "What are they doing so far from home?"

The Mino fought the impundulu, driving it away. But it was not without cost. One of the Mino, the woman with the spear, was killed. The other took up the spear but could not kill the creature. Thulani was relieved. If she had, he would have risked his life for nothing.

Thulani was about to stand when he felt the tip of something sharp prick the back of his neck. Whoever it was had approached him without him hearing a thing. He was impressed.

"I mean you no harm!" Thulani said.

"Bring me a torch!" the woman shouted.

Thulani heard the padding of bare feet against packed mud. The ground around him became visible as the torches arrived. He heard the woman growl as the sharp object pressed harder against his neck.

"A Zambulu sonchai!" the woman said. "I knew it! The Zambulu cursed us!"

"I am not responsible for this!" Thulani replied quickly, knowing that his life was in danger.

"If you weren't responsible, how do you know what I am talking about? How would you know about the killing storm?"

Thulani cleared his throat. "Because the same happened to a Zambulu village. I was tracking it and it led me here."

"Liar!"

The people attacked Thulani with their fists, sticks and stones. He curled up into a ball, wincing and whimpering with each blow.

"Stop!" the woman shouted. "We need him alive."

The beating halted and the villagers backed away.

"Stand up," the woman ordered.

Thulani stood, his hands raised.

"Turn around."

Thulani faced the woman. She was a Mino, her stout frame covered by ingwenya hide and chain mail armor. She held the spear and shield he saw in his vision. Though the spear was deadly, it was the shield that emitted a level of power that frightened him. Villagers with torches surrounded her, the intent on their faces clear. They wanted to kill him. The woman stepped toward him, leveling the spear at his throat.

"What was that thing that attacked us?" the woman asked.

"It is an impundulu," Thulani said. "When controlled by a sonchai it is harmless, but alone it becomes a powerful being capable of raising storms and killing people for their blood. It does not care if those people are Zambulu . . . or Matamban."

"So, you have come to claim it for your own?" the Mino asked.

"No," Thulani lied. "I have come to stop it."

"He's lying!" a person from the crowd shouted.

"Kill him!" said another.

The woman ignored them.

"You have the power to do so?"

"Yes."

The Mino gestured to the others with her head.

"Take his things and tie him up. We will hold him in the grain tower until morning."

A man and woman snatched Thulani's items away then tied his hands behind his back. They led him to the empty granary then shoved him inside, locking the metal gate behind him. The woman arrived a few moments later. She lowered her spear and shield.

"I am Izegbe, Petal of the Nkosa," she said. "Tomorrow, you will tell me how to kill this impundulu. If I am not satisfied with your words, I will kill you. Do you understand?"

"Yes," Thulani replied.

The woman stomped away. Thulani retreated into the granary, gathering straw for a makeshift bed. He smiled as he closed his eyes. He could have killed them all, but the warrior intrigued him. Her weapons were powerful and could help him subdue the impundulu. All he had to do was convince Izegbe that they had to work together. Once the creature was captured, he would dispose of her and return to the inkosi with his prize. He closed his eyes, the smile still on his face when sleep overwhelmed him.

-6-

Izegbe could not sleep. Her thoughts dwelled on Enomwoyi, the impundulu and the Zambulu sonchai, her emotions vacillating from anger to sorrow. Telling the Nkosa of Enomwoyi's death would be terrible but telling Enomowoyi's family would be far worse. She was their only daughter; losing her would be unbearable.

But the true pain was her own. Enomwoyi was more than a companion. They were just beginning to explore their true feelings for each other, which was why she asked her to accompany her home. And now she was dead, her spirit among the other Petals that had gone before them. It would be a lifetime before she saw her again.

Her sorrow transformed into anger again as she remembered the foul beast rising into the rain clouds as she looked on helpless. That anger deepened when she thought of the sonchai. She burst out of her hut, then strode to the granary. The sonchai was asleep atop a pile of straw. The sight of him lying peacefully while her friend and family lay dead made her furious. She unlocked the granary door, grabbed the sonchai by his feet then dragged him out.

"Wha . . .? What?" the sonchai exclaimed.

Izegbe rolled the man onto his back, sat on his chest then punched him in the face.

"This is your doing!" she shouted. "You did this!"

The sonchai tried to grab her hands as she pummeled him. She was about to hit him again for a seventh time when he pulled his arms to his body then thrust his hands toward her, his palms facing her.

"Hamba!" he shouted.

Izegbe flew into the air then landed on her back, her head striking the ground. She scrambled to her feet; the sonchai was standing, holding his bleeding nose.

"What is wrong with you?" he said. "I've done nothing to you."

"You are Zambulu," she said. "That is enough."

"Then why not let the villagers kill me?" the sonchai shot back.

"Because I need you to find that thing," she replied.

"I told you I would help you. This is unnecessary."

"It made me feel better," Izegbe replied.

"Why should I help you now?" the sonchai said. "I can find the impundulu myself. It's you that needs me. You would do well to remember that."

"You would not leave here alive."

The sonchai grinned. "And how would you stop me. You don't have your weapons with you."

Izegbe grinned as she held out her arm. Her shield appeared out of the darkness, the eyes of the face glowing. It slid onto her left arm. The sonchai backed away, his hands raised in submission.

"What a moment. Let's . . ."

She covered her body with the shield then spoke into it, smiling as an invisible force lifted the sonchai off his feet then tossed him back into the granary. She saw the sonchai's mouth move, but whatever spell he attempted to cast was drowned by Noxolo's voice. She pushed him against the granary wall, smiling as he grimaced.

"I'm sure if you had your other items, you would be a challenge," Izegbe said. "And as you said, I need you to find the beast. But understand that you live as long as you're useful. Defy me and you will die. I promise."

Izegbe whispered into the shield. The voice waned as she shut the granary door and locked it. She returned to her hut, her anger fed. She fell to sleep as soon as her head touched her head rest.

* * *

Morning came and Izegbe woke with renewed vigor. She donned her armor, gathered her weapons then went to the granary. Villagers congregated around the entrance; when they saw her their faces wrinkled with worry and fear.

"What is wrong?" she asked.

The chief approached her.

"The Zambulu sonchai is gone," he said.

"That's impossible! I visited him last night. I locked the door myself."

"You did," the chief replied. "But I think you forgot to tie his hands."

"I . . ."

Izegbe ran to the stables for her mbogo. She opened the gate to find Enomwoyi's bull gone. The damn sonchai had stolen it to make good his escape. She mounted her bull then kicked it into a full gallop. If the sonchai rode Enomwoyi's bull, he would stick to the main road. There was only one way for him to travel; the other way would lead him back to Zambululand.

Izegbe had only been in pursuit for a few minutes before she spotted her sister's bull and the sonchai. The Zambulu stood in front of the beast tugging its reins. He ceased when he saw Izegbe closing in. She thought he would run, but instead he remained in the road, his hands on his waist. Izegbe took a throwing spear from her sheath. She threw the spear, hoping to wound the sonchai in his thigh. To her surprise he caught it and threw it back at her. The spear barely missed her head. Izegbe pulled her bull's reins, bringing it to a halt. She dismounted, Enomwoyi's spear in her right hand, Noxolo on her left arm.

"You caught my spear," she said.

"You are a poor thrower," the sonchai replied. "I may not be a warrior, but I am Zambulu."

"Why didn't you run?" she asked.

"This bull is stupid," the sonchai said. "And there was no need to. I thought if I got you away from the village we could talk rationally."

"What do you wish to say?"

"There is no reason for us to be enemies," the sonchai replied. "Your shield has great power. It would be helpful protecting us from the impundulu in its full form. I have the means to find it and subdue it. If we work together, we can capture it much easier."

"I'm not interested in capturing it," Izegbe replied. "I'm going to kill it."

"So, we don't agree on everything," the sonchai said. "Let's take one step at a time. First, we find it, then we will decide what to do with it."

Izegbe lowered her spear. It was true that she could not find the creature without the sonchai's help. The plan was to force him to help her find the creature, then kill both. Having him as an ally would make her task less demanding. She had no reason to trust him, but she decided to take the chance for an opportunity to avenge Enomwoyi and her family's death.

"Get on the mbogo," she said. "You lead."

The sonchai smiled. He trotted to the bull then mounted him.

"How do I get it to go?" he said.

"How did you do it in the village?"

"I struck it on the head. It ran to get rid of me."

Izegbe rolled her eyes. This fool was not worthy of Enomwoyi's bull. "Take the reins in your hands, then press your heels against its body."

The sonchai followed Izegbe's instructions and the bull lumbered down the road. He lifted his gourd; the object emitted a green glow.

"This way," he said.

Izegbe nudged her bull and followed, keeping a wary eye on her new companion, and hoping she had not made a bad decision. For a moment she thought of killing him and taking the gourd, but knowing the sonchai and his tricks, the calabash would not work unless he possessed it. She resigned herself to his company until the impundulu was found and killed.

They travelled the remainder of the day, making good use of the sunlight. They rested at a small river, wary of the mambas patrolling the water's edge. No words passed between them, each in their own thoughts. Izegbe attempted to sleep, but the terror of recent days kept invading her dreams. She looked across the path at the sonchai; he lay against a tree, sleeping peacefully. Anger rose in her throat, but she pushed it down. If his words were true, it was not his fault Enomwoyi and the others were dead. Still, it was Zambulu ashé that created this - what did he call it? -impundulu. It wouldn't exist if it wasn't for those like him. Her hand went to her sword. She squeezed its hilt, soothed by its warm ivory composition. After at time she let it go. Discipline would allow her to achieve her goal. She leaned against the tree, and finally found a peaceful slumber.

-7-

Thulani waited until he was sure the Mino slept before sitting up to check his gourd. The embers inside pulsed brightly. They were going in the right direction, but they still had a good distance to travel. Long stops like this would not help them make up time, especially since he had no idea where the impundulu headed. A bird under the control of a sonchai would have a purpose, traveling directly to where it was sent. But this was a rogue fowl, seeking nourishment wherever it sensed it. Its former master probably shared his own blood, which accounted for the powerful storms it spawned. If they were lucky, the sustenance it received from random victims would eventually weaken it, but that was uncertain. Thulani had no experience raising an impundulu, so he had no way of knowing for sure.

He stood then crept to the Mino. She lay under her shield, her companion's spear just beyond her outstretched hand. Thulani closed his eyes as he extended his fly whisk toward the weapons. He yelped; the whisk's handle burned against his flesh like fire. He dropped it on the ground and the grass caught fire. And then Izegbe was awake, the spear in her hand, the tip of its broadleaf inches from his throat.

"What are you doing, sonchai!?!?"

Thulani stumbled away, his hands raised in submission.

"Nothing! I was just . . ."

Izegbe kicked Thulani in the chest, knocking him to the ground. She walked to the burning grass then stomped it out. She picked up Enomwoyi's spear. Thulani grimaced as she pressed the spearhead tip into his chest.

"I'd kill you if I didn't need you," she said. "Your head would make a great gift for Enomwoyi's family."

Izegbe backed away. "Stand up and turn around."

Thulani obeyed. Izegbe put down her shield then took a length of twine from her shoulder pack. She tied Thulani's hands behind his back.

"Mino, this is not necessary," he said.

"Apparently it is," Izegbe replied. "Now go to your tree and let me sleep."

Izegbe watched until he leaned against the tree then slid to the ground. Satisfied he would cause no more trouble, she settled into a fitful rest.

* * *

Izegbe and Thulani continued their journey after daybreak. They stopped at noon to eat and rest, then continued down narrow paths and open fields, through dense forests and open savanna, following the erratic path of the impundulu. They were approaching a wide river when Izegbe's eyes widened.

"Stop!" she shouted.

Thulani reined his bull still.

"What is the matter?" he asked.

"We cannot cross this river," Izegbe replied.

"Why?" Thulani asked. "We're told your war bulls are bred from the water mbogo, which mean they can swim."

Thulani attempted to shade his eyes from the sun but remembered his hands were bound, so he squinted.

"I see no mambas or kibokos."

"That river is the border between Matamba and Asanteman," Izegbe said. "We cannot cross."

"You cannot cross," Thulani said. "I'm Zambulu. We have no quarrel with Asanteman."

"Everyone has a quarrel with Asanteman, whether they know it or not."

Thulani shrugged. "No matter. Free my hands and give me my gourd and your shield. With both I can capture the impundulu alone."

Izegbe shook her head. "The Noxolo will not Speak for you. And I will not let you take this abomination and my shield back to your inkosi."

"Then free my hands so I can return to Zambululand. I will tell my inkosi that I could not capture the impundulu, but it is of no concern to us because it finds Matambans and Asantahe more to its liking."

Izegbe dismounted then took out her knife. Thulani closed his eyes, expected to be killed. Instead, she cut his hands free and gave him back his gourd. The sonchai sighed in relief as he jumped off the mbogo.

"Take it back to your companion's family," he said. "I won't need it."

Izegbe stared at Thulani, emotions raging inside. She knew her presence in Asanteman could spark a war, but she was not about to be shamed by a lowly Zambulu sonchai.

"Get back on the mbogo," she said. "We continue."

Thulani smirked and mounted his mbogo. Together they crossed the river into Asanteman.

"We'll stay off the roads and avoid cities or villages," Izegbe said.

"That will be hard to do," Thulani replied. "I don't know this land. I must follow the path the impundulu leaves."

"Then you'll have to," Izegbe said. "I won't be the start of another war."

"You already are."

The Asanteman warriors emerged from the nearby foliage with a suddenness that startled the mbogos. Izegbe managed to control her bovine, but Thulani was thrown from his, landing awkwardly on his side. The bull disappeared into the bush. The gourd struck the ground and broke, the glowing gris-gris spilling out.

Twenty Asanteman border guards surrounded them, covered in thick kapok armor and brandishing long spears and leaf shields. Izegbe reined her mbogo back to Izegbe, who remained on the ground in a daze. Izegbe cursed herself for her error. She should have known the Asanteman would be watching the borders; the war had recently ended, but emotions still ran high.

A warrior wearing layers of gold necklaces approached, a menacing look on his umber face.

"The Asantehene was correct," he said. "The Matambans are not to be trusted. Not only do they violate our borders, but they also send a Petal!"

Izegbe remained silent as she assessed the danger. The only warrior worthy of her iron was the one circling her. The others were probably local militia, unskilled and unreliable. But their numbers could not be underestimated. She looked at Thulani, still lying on the ground. If he was not injured, he might be of some help.

"Shut up, dog man," Izegbe said. She closed her eyes, her left hand tightening on her shield handle.

"Noxolo!"

Her shield responded, its eyes snapping open. It released a howl that sent the Asanteman flying backwards, his armor split at the chest. Izegbe leaped off her mbogo, lunging at the opening in the torn armor with her spear. Despite being caught off guard, the Asanteman managed to parry the attack with his sword as the others converged on Izegbe. The war bull instinctively took a stance behind her, protecting her back. Izegbe deflected their attacks with shield and spear, waiting as Noxolo regains its strength for another attack.

Izegbe heard the mbogo bellow behind her. She looked up to see Thulani running toward her, his face tight with fear.

"Get down!" he yelled.

He slammed into her before she could think. She lay on the ground stunned as Thulani grabbed Noxolo and pulled it over them.

"We can't hide . . ."

Intense light blinded her despite being covered by the shield. Thunder drummed on the metal, shaking them both. The lighting flashed again and again, the thunder beating them like drum skins. Then the lightning ceased, and silence prevailed. The smell of burnt flesh seeped under the shield. Izegbe began pushing the shield aside and Thulani grabbed her hand.

"Slowly," he cautioned.

Izegbe nodded. She slid the shield aside; she and Thulani stood, protecting themselves behind the shield. They saw the bodies of the Asanteman, smoke rising from where the lightning struck them. Her mbogo was dead as well, its bulk struck numerous times. Thulani scanned the area, and then he saw it.

"By the ancestors!" he whispered.

The impundulu strutted a few strides away, its white plumage glistening with illuminous light streaks flowing like waves over its body. It seemed to hover over a particular spot, pecking at the ground gently. It took Thulani a few moments to realize what it was doing.

"The gris-gris," he said.

"What?" Izegbe asked.

"The gris-gris, the objects I used to follow it. It seems when I spilled it, it summoned the impundulu."

"You mean that's all we had to do?" Izegbe said. She shoved the sonchai.

"I didn't know," Thulani replied. "My knowledge of it is limited.

A small explosion occurred near them. They looked up to see the impundulu staring at them, its long head tilted as if contemplating their fate. They withdrew behind the shield.

"It's confused," Thulani said. "It's been summoned, but it doesn't know by whom."

He took his knife from his waist then cut his palm.

"What are you doing?" Izegbe said.

"Feeding it," he replied.

"If you step from behind Noxolo, it will kill you."

"It might, but then it might not," Thulani said. "Why would you care?"

Izegbe didn't reply. Thulani grinned.

"I thought so."

Thulani emerged from behind Noxolo, his palm open for the impundulu to see. If the stories were correct, this was how a sonchai fed their familiar. If he was wrong, he would soon be able to discuss it with the ancestors. The impundulu straightened then flashed. It lowered its head then walked hesitantly toward him. It stopped a few steps from him and Thulani stood still. The creature extended its beak, pecking at his hand but not touching it. Then its tongue flicked from its beak, licking his blood. Thulani felt a tingle course through his body. The tongue touched his palm again, but this time the sensation was less intense. The impundulu relaxed, folding its long legs under its torso and sitting on the ground. It belonged to him now, the most powerful impundulu ever encountered. Thulani imagined the inkosi rewarding him with cattle and land for bringing him such a powerful talisman. He squatted beside the bird, touching its crown. A soft rumbling sound came from its throat, and it shifted closer to him.

The impundulu jerked then emitted a piercing scream. Thulani was doused with brightness and pain. He collapsed onto his side, paralyzed. It took a few moments for his eyes to clear. When they did, he saw a horrible sight. The impundulu stumbled about, a spear protruding from his body. The weapon had not penetrated deep, but it was enough to cling to the bird. Thulani's head burned with anger. He spun about, expecting to see Izegbe's triumphant smile. Instead, he saw the Petal sprawled on the ground, her enchanted shield and spear on the ground beside her. Standing before her was the Asanteman leader. The right side of his face was singed, as was his arm. He held another spear ready to throw.

Thulani ran toward him as fast as his wounded body would allow. The warrior threw the spear and Thulani caught it. He reversed the weapon then threw it back at the warrior. He was not as fast as Izegbe. The spear pierced the warrior's throat and he fell to his knees clutching the shaft. Thulani ran to Izegbe's side. There was a wound to the back of her head from the warrior's club. He looked to the impundulu, the bird still reeling.

"By the Cleave!" he exclaimed.

He opened his bag, taking out the necessary concoctions to treat Izegbe's wound while watching the impundulu struggle with the spear. As he cleaned Izegbe's wound the bird shook the spear free then stumbled to a nearby body. It pecked the skin until a steady stream of blood flowed. The creature lapped the fluid, and as it did its wound healed.

Thulani finished bandaging Izegbe's wound as the impundulu's cut healed. When Thulani's eyes met the bird's, he knew he was in danger. The bond between them was broken. Flickers of light appeared in the bird's plumage as its body stiffened. Thulani scrambled to Izegbe's shield then covered them.

"Noxolo!" he shouted.

The shield's voice appeared as the stream of lightning bolts reached them. The force knocked him backwards, but he locked his knees and steading himself. The attack subsided and the impundulu let out an ear-piercing scream before leaping into the sky and flying away.

Thulani watched it disappear into the cloudless sky, his dreams fading with it.

"Sonchai?"

Izegbe was attempting to sit up. Thulani ambled to her and pressed her back down.

"Rest," he said. "You're wounded."

Izegbe nodded.

"Where is the impundulu?" she asked.

"Gone," Thulani answered.

"Is it dead?"

Thulani shook his head. "The Asanteman attempted to kill it. He came close."

Izegbe touched the bandage on her head then winced.

"Who did this? You?"

"Of course," Thulani replied.

Izegbe's shoulders slumped. "I was going to kill the lightning bird, and you still helped me?"

Thulani shrugged. "Your loss fueled your anger. I understand. Besides, we have fought together. That makes us cohorts, doesn't it?"

They heard a snort. The other mbogo wandered into the clearing and began chewing grass, oblivious to the carnage around it.

"Let's get you back across the river," he said.

He went to the bovine, grabbed its reins then led it to Izegbe. After securing her weapons and robbing the dead Asantemen of their supplies, they set out for the river.

"What about the impundulu," Izegbe asked. "Will it die from its wounds?"

"No," Thulani replied. "It healed itself as I healed you."

"Will you be able to find it again?"

"I don't know. I'll have to return to Zambululand, to the place where it was created and gather more gris gris."

Izegbe nodded. "I will go back to Matamba and take Enomwoyi's possessions to her family. I must return her spear to the Ngola. A new Petal must be initiated."

They reached the river. The crossing was easy; no Asanteman border guards waited to thwart them.

"You should be fine now," Thulani said.

"Wait," she said. "How did you protect us from the impundulu."

"I used your shield," Thulani said.

Izegbe's eyes narrowed. "How?"

Thulani looked thoughtful. "I called Noxolo . . ."

"And she answered?"

Thulani's eyes widened. "Yes. What does that mean?"

"I don't know," Izegbe admitted. "Do you intend to continue to seek the lightning bird?"

"Yes," Thulani answered.

Izegbe lowered her head in contemplation. The sonchai had saved her life, and like he said, they had fought together. There was no stronger bond that battle. When she raised her head, her face reflected her resolve.

"I will help you," Izegbe said.

Thulani's eyes went wide. "What?"

"It is my fault that you did not succeed," she said. "I must help you to regain my honor. And if Noxolo answered your call, there must be something more to your journey."

"And you will not try to kill it again?"

Izegbe laughed. "I don't think so, but I cannot promise that I won't try. Come with me to Matamba. I will settle my business, then we will find your impundulu."

"So be it," Thulani said. "Are you sure your Ngola will accept a lowly Zambulu?"

Izegbe smiled. "I will make her."

Thulani grinned. "The word of a Petal is good enough for this old sonchai. Let's go."

Together they waded across the river to Matamba.

Betta Listen

The house wasn't much but it was all he could afford. Stephanie told him a hundred times they needed more life insurance, but he didn't listen. Life insurance was for old people; they were still in their thirties and in great shape. Nothing could or would happen to them.

Randolph Chambers followed the moving truck up the steep driveway then thought better of it. They would need room to take out the furniture, what little there was. Instead he parked the SUV on the curb. Steph's chemo drained everything they had and then some. What little he was able to keep was augmented by donations from family and friends. They should have counted themselves lucky, but they didn't. Randolph would rather live on the streets with Steph and Gina than in a mansion alone.

"So, this is home now?" Gina barely looked up from her cellphone. It was their last luxury, a gift from a co-worker.

"Yeah, baby girl, this is home."

"Uh huh." Randolph heard her shift in her seat, but he didn't look at her. It was hard for him to. He hated to see the disappointment in her face and the pain that lingered just beneath it. She looked so much like her mother, her gestures and expressions a reflection of Stephanie. He gathered himself and turned to her, forcing a smile on his face.

"Come on. Let's go see what our little bit of money bought us."

He shifted the Explorer into park and exited. He was halfway up the driveway when he noticed Gina was still in the SUV. He walked back and tapped on her window. She looked at him, raising her eyebrows in annoyance.

"Roll down the window," he said.

The window slid down.

"Aren't you coming?"

Gina rolled her eyes. "It's just a house. It's not home."

Randolph ignored the insult, just as he'd done every day since Stephanie died. The psychiatrist said it was normal for children to act out after a parent's death, so he sucked it in and took the blows. Some days it was harder than others.

Stephanie climbed out and they trudged up the driveway and into the house. Randolph had hoped his opinion of the modest home would change after a few weeks, but it didn't. He should have been thankful to be in a house at all, but he wasn't. Everything was less now.

He forced a smile. "Why don't you go pick out your room?"

Gina stared at the floor. "It doesn't matter."

"Well pick out mine then."

Gina cut him a curious glance. "Sure, whatever." She stomped up the stairs.

Randolph stepped aside as the movers brought in the great room furniture and sat it down in the room to his right. He went down the narrow hallway into the kitchen/dinette area and did a quick inspection. He'd have to replace the faucets when he got paid. The laundry room was a cramped space that barely accommodated the stacked washer and dryer, but it would do.

"Daddy!"

Randolph broke his musing and trotted upstairs. "What's up, baby girl?"

"I'm in here."

Randolph entered the first room. Gina sat on the floor in the corner, a serious look on her face.

"This is it. This is my room."

Randolph looked about the empty space and frowned. It was the smallest room in the house; her furniture wouldn't fit. He'd have to put her chest of drawers in another room or the basement.

"You sure you want this . . ."

"I'm sure. It feels right. This is my room."

Randolph shrugged and walked out. He knew it wasn't the right response, but he didn't care. He was tired, physically and mentally. He'd be a better father tomorrow.

He spent the next three hours leading the movers around the house making sure everything was in its proper place. He wouldn't have much help arranging furniture once they left. Most of his friends were really Stephanie's friends. After the mandatory support period they all slowly disappeared. His real friends lived in his hometown of Atlanta, too far away to drop by and lend a hand. Stacy Upchurch, his best friend, had promised to fly out to visit 'as soon as he got settled,' but Stacy was never settled.

The movers arranged Gina's furniture around her. She sat in the corner of the room, eyes closed and head bobbing to whatever played on her cellphone.

"Where do you want your bed?" he asked.

"I don't care," Gina replied.

"Set it by the window," Randolph told the movers.

"No!" Gina jumped to her feet, her expression angry.

"Anywhere but there."

Randolph had enough. "Take off those damn earphones!"

Gina glared at him then slowly removed them.

Randolph folded his arms. "Now you're going to tell these hard-working men where you want your furniture and you're going to do it politely. And if you snap at me one more time, I'm going to snatch that cellphone and throw it into the street. You understand?"

Gina nodded her head.

"Do you understand?"

Gina looked away. "Yes, sir."

Randolph stormed out of the room. When the movers were done, he paid them then went to his own room. He'd sold the king size bed and replaced it with a queen. It was too big, but that wasn't the reason he sold it. Stephanie loved that bed with its tall rice posts, standing so high from the floor she needed a step stool to climb into it. She used to say it made her feel like a child to sit on it, her feet dangling over the edge. The bed even smelled like her, or at least her favorite perfume. When he slept in the old bed her memories awakened. So he sold it not because he wanted to, but because he had to. That was when things between him and Gina started going bad. She accused him of trying to forget Stephanie. He couldn't get her to understand that he wasn't trying to forget. He just couldn't have her memories so close.

The good thing about the new/old house was that it was still in Gina's school district. The bad thing was that Randolph had to drive her to school. It wouldn't have been a problem before. He was a street salesman before Stephanie took ill and he could arrange his calls around his personal life. Once Stephanie was diagnosed, he took an inside sales position. It was less money and he hated sitting at a desk all day, but he needed to be close to make sure she made her treatments and to help around the house. Having to take Gina to school meant getting up earlier, and Randolph was not a morning person. But that didn't matter. This was life now. It would have to do.

* * *

Gina stomped down the hallway the next morning and dropped into her chair. Randolph did a finishing flourish with the scrambled eggs then slid a portion on her plate. He scooped a spoonful of grits beside the eggs the placed two pieces of bacon on the edge.

"Good morning!" he said.

"Yeah," Gina replied. Randolph would have been shocked if she had said more.

She attacked the food like a starving child as he made his own plate and sat opposite her.

"So how was your first night in the new room?"

"Terrible," she mumbled.

Randolph nodded. "The first night in a new house can be rough."

"It was all that noise."

Randolph mixed his eggs and grits. "What noise?"

"All that talking. I guess it was the neighbors. You didn't hear it?"

"No." Randolph glanced at the clock. "Shit...I mean, darn it. It's almost time to go. Hurry up."

"I just got here!" Gina whined.

"It's either ride or walk," Randolph retorted.

Gina scooped up her food. "You need to talk to the neighbors. They're too loud."

"I will. Now let's get you to school and me to work."

Randolph sped to the school and joined the parent processional. He was two cars away from the drop off point when Tanisha Bridges emerged from the building. The young pretty assistant principal came straight for their car.

"Not today," Randolph whispered. "I don't have time for this."

She walked up to the passenger door, flashing her bright smile and waving as if they were a mile away. Gina opened the door and stepped onto the curb. She was immediately swallowed into Tanisha's hug.

"Welcome back, Gina! We missed you!"

"Yeah," Gina replied. She escaped Tanisha's embrace and trudged to the school building.

Tanisha turned her attention to Randolph.

"How is everything, Randolph?" she asked with over exaggerated concern.

"As good as can be expected," Randolph replied.

"These things take time, Randolph. Is it okay if I call you Randolph?"

Hell no!

"It's fine, Ms. Bridges."

"Please, call me Tanisha."

The tenor of her smile changed, its intention matching her words.

"I'd love to talk — why did he say that- but I'm late for work." Randolph shifted the Explorer into drive.

"I understand Randolph We'll talk soon." She closed the door and waved, mouthing the words, Have a nice day.

Randolph crept to the stoplight at the entrance of the school then into traffic. Steph was right. Ms.

Barnes-Tanisha-did have a crush on him. She would tease him during PTO meetings about how she would look him up and down and giggle like a twelve-year-old whenever he said something witty. It was funny then, but not now. Now she seemed like a vulture, waiting to swoop down on the remains of their marriage. He debated whether to curse her out the next time he saw her.

He pulled into the parking lot ten minutes late. As he snuck into the side entrance he encountered Taylor Freemen, his boss, standing before the coffee dispenser filling his cup. He cut an eye at Randolph then at the break room clock.

"Morning, Randy," he said coolly.

"Good morning."

Randolph hurried by him. He went directly to his cubicle and sat in front of his computer. He was logging in when Taylor appeared over him.

"How it going?" he asked.

"Fine,"

"How's Gina doing?"

"Fine."

"Is there anything I can do?"

"No."

Taylor lingered and the moment became awkward. Randolph waited for him to say it. Taylor wasn't a tactful man, so his hesitance was out of character. He'd seen his boss rake other employees over the coals for taking too much bereavement time. But Randolph was different. He was the company's best salesman when he was on the road and now, he was its best in-house sale rep. Firing him meant losing money and Taylor hated losing money. It wasn't that Randolph's work was bad; he was still closing deals head over heels compared to the other reps, he just wasn't producing Randolph numbers.

Taylor scratched his balding head. "Well, if you need to talk or anything, let me know. We're . . . I mean I'm here to help. You're a valuable employee and I know things are tough right now. We want to see you back to your old self."

"So I can get back to making you money."

"Sure, thanks Taylor. I really appreciate it."

Randolph logged in and went through the motions of the day. On his worst day he was better than most, and the past few weeks were his worst days. Before Steph's illness he was road warrior, a street salesman bouncing from city to city and sometimes state to state hawking TF's electronic goods. But he requested an inside job when she was diagnosed. Upper management resisted until he threatened to quit.

He ate lunch at his desk. On his screen a string of memories scrolled by, images of his life during better times. Photos of Hilton Head spring vacations, summers in Canada and winters in Key West marched by in perfect time, triggering as much joy as pain. He watched the pictures flash by repeatedly. He was still watching them when his phone rang. It was another wasted day.

"Hello?" His voice was almost angry when he answered.

"Randolph, this is Tanisha. We need you to come to the school immediately. There's an issue with Gina."

"I'll be right there." Randolph hung up the phone before Tanisha could explain. He grabbed his things and rushed toward the door.

"Hey, hey hold up partner!" Taylor yelled. "Where are you running to? You just got here."

"Trouble at my daughter's school," Randolph shouted back. "I'll be in early tomorrow."

He sped to the school. Tanisha waited outside.

"What's going on, Tanisha?"

"Gina was in a fight."

"Fight? Gina's never been in a fight in her life! What happened? Was someone picking on her? You know she's . . ."

"Calm down, Randolph." Tanisha placed a comforting hand on his shoulder. He flinched then cut his eyes at Tanisha. She took her hand away.

"Gina started the fight. She's in the principal's office right now. As much as I hate it, we have to suspend her for two days."

Randolph nodded absently. "I understand."

"Will there be anyone at home with her?"

"I'll take the days off," he said immediately, knowing he'd catch hell from Taylor.

"I'll figure out some way to work from home."

"Follow me."

Randolph followed Tanisha through the narrow halls to the principal's office. Gina sat by the door. Her clothes were crumpled, and a dark bruise had formed around her left eye. He knelt in front of her.

"You alright, baby girl?"

Gina nodded. "Don't call me that."

"Mr. Chambers?"

Randolph turned to see Principal Wiggins approaching him. He shook the principal's hand, wincing as the tall ex-football player squeezed a bit too hard.

"I'm sorry we have to meet under such circumstances," Wiggins said. "Gina's usually a good young lady. This is as much a surprise to us, as I'm sure it is to you."

"It is," Randolph said. He was angry and embarrassed.

"I wish we could handle this situation differently due to Gina's circumstances, but rules are rules. We have to suspend her."

Gina's circumstances? So, Stephanie's death was just circumstances to them.

"As I told Ms. Bridges, I understand."

He went back to Gina. "Come on, let's go."

Gina followed him to the car. They rode home in silence. Randolph didn't know what to say. He was angry at her for fighting, but he knew it had something to do with Stephanie. She should be punished, but how would she take it? He couldn't do it any longer. It was time to talk to a therapist. No matter how he tried he couldn't make it right on his own. The pain went deep like old roots.

He was still coming to a stop in the driveway when Gina flung open the car door then jumped out. She was fumbling with her keys at the door by the time he exited the car.

"Gina?"

She shoved open the door then went inside. Randolph followed her to her room. When he entered, she was on the bed crying. He tried to speak to her, searching his mind for a string of comforting words to say but he came up empty. The truth was he wanted to do the same thing, but he couldn't. He was her father. He had to be strong for her. So, he placed his hand on her until she sat up, hugging him until she fell asleep in his arms. He lay her down then slipped to his room. He took a long, hot shower, trying his best to wash the tension from his body and mind. But his mind wouldn't give in. He sat in front of the television, flipping channels before giving up then listening to Al Jarreau until he became drowsy. He decided to check on Gina before calling it a night.

Randolph managed to get the days off and, as expected, his boss wasn't happy. But it was more important to be available for Gina. He spent most of his day researching therapists when he wasn't cooking meals. He tried to talk to Gina about the school incident, but she wouldn't say much.

"Some stupid kid said something they shouldn't have," was her reply.

At night he would walk to her room and hear her talking to her friends. At least she was sharing with someone. Once he found a good therapist, things would change. Or so he hoped.

Friday night Randolph had enough of cooking. He decided they would splurge and go to their favorite Chinese restaurant, Tao. It was a good drive away, but the food was worth it.

"Gina!" he called out. "Let's go out!"

There was no answer.

"Gina?"

Randolph put on his polo shirt and jeans then headed for Gina's room. He heard voices halfway down the hallway. At first, he thought Gina might be on the phone with one of her friends, but as he listened closely, he realized it wasn't her voice. It was a collection of voices, children and adults, male and female. He went to the window at the end of the hallway then peered outside; the streets were empty. Walking back to Gina's door he was sure the voices came from her room. He opened the door.

Gina sat on the floor beside the wall, a blank look on her face. Behind her the wall writhed with dozens of faces, their mouths spewing a torrent of words. Randolph lunged toward Gina, but something shoved him back.

"Betta listen!" the voices said in unison. *"Bring him back. Bring him back. Bring him back!"*

A bright light emerged from the wall surrounding Gina. She began to fade.

"No!" Randolph tried to reach her again, but he was shoved back. He watched as she faded then disappeared.

"Bring him back. You get her back. Betta listen!"

The last thing he saw of Gina was her eyes. Then the light and the faces were gone. He was alone in her room.

"Gina! Gina!" Randolph snatched open her closest. He looked under her bed. He ran through the house, searching every room as his voice went raw screaming her name. Then went back to her room, collapsing on the floor before the wall where she disappeared.

"Betta listen," the voices whispered. *"Bring the man back."*

"What man?" Randolph croaked.

"The man that lived here. The man that killed us."

He'd gone mad, he thought. The strain of Stephanie's death had driven him insane. Gina was somewhere in the house hiding from him, probably terrified of him.

"Gina, stop hiding and come on out," he said. "I'm okay."

"I'm not hiding, daddy," he heard her whisper. *"I'm with them."*

"It's going to be alright baby," he said. "Don't worry, it's going to be alright."

Randolph ran back to his room. He had no idea who owned this house before. He rummaged through his top dresser drawer until he found the

Sunshine Realty card. He punched the numbers on his phone with trembling fingers.

"This Ann Coolidge," the sweet southern voice said.

"Ann, this is Randolph, Randolph Chambers. You sold me the house in the Old Fourth Ward."

"Oh yes, Mr. Chambers! How is everything?"

"It's fine. Ann, I was wondering if you knew the person that owned this house previously."

There was silence for a moment. "Yes, I do. His name is Charles Wynn. He bought a house in Griffin. A small thing with a lot of land."

"He left a few things at the house. I'd like to ship them to him. Do you have the address?"

"Yes, I do. That's kind of you. Most people would just count it as a bonus. I'll email you the information tomorrow."

"I was wondering if you could send it tonight." Randolph struggled to keep his desperation out of his voice.

"Well, okay. Give me a minute. Nice talking to you Randolph."

"Same here, Ann."

Randolph hung up then gazed at his screen. It took Ann thirty minutes to email the address. He immediately pulled up his GPS app then plugged in the address. As the GPS did its job, he went into his closet then opened the safe. Inside was a 9mm Glock and a Taser. The Taser was Stephanie's; she refused to carry a gun. He took both weapons.

Randolfh grabbed a coat and hat then hurried downstairs to the garage. There he found a roll of duct tape. Not once did he hesitate, not once did he have second thoughts. He had to find Gina.

By the time he got in the car the directions to Charles Wynn's house were plotted. He sped out of the neighborhood headed for Griffin, Georgia. The drive took him longer than he thought it would. By the time he reached the Highway 16 exit he was low on gas. He stopped, filling the tank at a roadside gas station. The GPS guided him down a dark lightless road bordered by pines and oaks, the shadowy wall of vegetation occasionally interrupted by farms or small homesteads.

"You have reached your destination," the GPS announced.

Randolph stopped his car before the open area. The grass rose high against the ragged barb wire fence, a damaged light flickering over the driveway entrance. The house stood about fifty yards from the road, so faking a broken-down car wouldn't work. He cut off his lights then drove up to the house. There was no pretense to his actions; he had no time for such things and had no idea what he was doing.

He banged on the door. Hard footsteps advanced the stopped. The door jerked open.

Charles Wynn stood about Randolph's height but was powerfully built. A ragged beard covered his pale, pockmarked face. He glared at Randolph with bloodshot blue eyes.

"Who are you? What the hell are you doing here? What do you want?"

Randolph pulled out his gun with a shaky hand.

"I need you to come with me," he said.

Charles knocked the gun from his hand. It struck the porch then went off, shattering the nearby window. He grabbed Randolph's coat, jerked him inside then threw him across the room. Randolph crashed against the wall, blacking out for a moment.

"How did you find out?" Charles barked. "How?"

Randolph's sight cleared to Charles coming at him with a knife. The blade was covered with blood. Randolph checked himself; it wasn't his. He looked about desperately then saw someone lying on the couch. It was a man, his eyes staring blankly into the ceiling. Blood ran down his shirt then dripped onto the brown carpet. Randolph pushed back his fear, waiting for the murderer to come to him.

"Don't matter how you found out," he said. "Don't matter at all.'"

Randolph waited until Charles reached for him. He slapped the man's hand aside then drove the Taser into his chest and pressed the button. Charles shook, dropping the knife then collapsing to the floor. Randolph waited until he stopped convulsing then scrambled to his feet. He tased him until he knew he was unconscious then ran outside to his car for the duct tape. Randolph fought to ignore the dead man on the couch, concentrating on his task. He taped Charles' feet together then taped his hands behind his back. He taped his mouth last.

With a grunt Randolph lifted Charles from the floor then tried to lift him onto his shoulder. He was too heavy. Instead he gripped Charles under the arms and dragged him to the car. Randolph made sure no one watched before opening the car trunk and putting Charles inside. He jumped in the car then sped away, driving back to the city. He waited until he was almost home before calling the Griffin police and reporting the dead man.

Randolph pulled into the garage then closed the door. When he opened the trunk Charles was conscious. There was no fear in his eyes, just anger.

Randolph reached for him, but Charles rolled away, kicking at him with his bound legs. Randolph took out the Taser; Charles pleaded with his eyes just before Randolph tased him. He waited a moment then lifted him from the trunk. Randolph struggled up the stairs, praying that none of the neighbors saw him carrying the man into the house. By the time he reached the inside stairs he was exhausted. He grabbed Charles's feet then dragged him up, the man's head bouncing off each step. He continued to drag him into Gina's room then collapsed on his ass exhausted. He glared at the wall.

"He's here!" he shouted.

Faint mumbling danced about him.

"Where's my daughter?" he shouted.

"He's here!" the voices shouted.

The faces appeared on the walls full of ecstatic smiles. The light that consumed Gina materialized over Charles. The killer came to as the light descended on him, his screams muffled by the tape, his jerking motions telegraphing the extreme pain he suffered. The faces laughed in delight as their brightness enveloped him, their glee increasing with each tortured scream. Then the light exploded, blinding Randolph and knocking him on his back. When his sight cleared Gina lay on the floor before him.

Randolph sat up and grabbed her, hugging her tight as tears streamed from his eyes.

"Daddy?" she said.

"Yes, baby, it's Daddy."

She hugged him back. "I saw momma."

Randolph pulled away from her. "What?"

"I saw momma. She told me to tell you that she loves and misses us. She told me to tell you not to worry. We'll be together again."

He looked in Gina's eyes. She was calm, her eyes peaceful.

Randolph hugged her again.

"Everything is going to be alright baby girl," he said. "It's going to be alright."

"I know daddy," Gina whispered. "I know. You listened."

Slipping into Darkness

'I was slippin' into darkness,
When they took my friend away.
I was slipping into darkness,
When they took...when they took my friend
away.
You know he loved to drink good whiskey,
While laughing at the moon.

Slipping into Darkness by War

Zeke grabbed the full shot glass with trembling fingers as the patrons of the Luna Oscura saloon chanted.

"Bwé, bwé, bwé . . ."

The saloon blurred, so he blinked his eyes to clear his vision. Josué stared at him, a jovial smile between his round dimpled cheeks on his ebony face.

"Come on, mon frère! One more shot and the eagles are ours!"

"Easy for you to say," Zeke slurred. "You ain't drinkin'."

Zeke steadied his hand then slowly raised the shot glass to his mouth. He drank slowly, the brown liquid burning a path between his puckered lips and teeth down to his churning stomach. He closed his eyes then slammed the glass on the table. Zeke swayed and everyone gasped; He steadied then opened his eyes as he grinned.

"How's that for a Freedonian!" he shouted.

His comrades and the saloon patrons answered his words with curses and applause. Josué took off his beret and collected their winnings. He dropped the hat on the table before Zeke.

"Not bad, mon frère, not bad at all!"

"Told you I could do it," Zeke said.

"There's enough here to put us in high style for the next week!"

"Too bad we muster out in three days," Zeke replied.

"We'll blow it when we get to New Orleans," Josué said.

"Josué!"

His friend turned toward the saloon entrance. A well-dressed man and woman with serious expressions entered, both glaring at Josué. When he turned back his face was serious.

"Zeke, I have business to tend to," he said. "I'll be back."

"I'm coming with you," Zeke said. "We're supposed to be celebrating, remember?"

"I'll be just a minute," Josué said.

"Bullshit!"

Zeke stood as the couple approached the table. By their clothing he could tell they were Spaniards, which made him suspicious.

"Aren't you going to introduce me?" Zeke said.

"Another time," Josué said.

Zeke stepped toward his friend and his head spun. His stomach roiled like a flooding river and his eyes became heavy.

"Oh shit," he said.

As his eyesight faded, he saw Josué, the man and the woman walk through the saloon doors into the darkness.

* * *

The squeaking of the awakening soldiers' bunks dug into Zeke's ears like a broken bugle. He sat up to cover his ears and his head spun like a twister, so he lay back down then belched the nasty taste of sour whiskey into his mouth.

"My Lord," he moaned.

Zeke sat up slower the second time, the spinning still present but manageable. He stood then staggered out of the room, ignoring the jibes and complaints of his comrades. By the time he reached the latrine the foul concoction in his stomach had worked its way into his throat. He barely made it to the toilet. After a gut-wrenching vomit, he felt better. Zeke rinsed out his mouth then ambled back to the room for his shaving kit. As he approached his bunk, he noticed Josué's empty bed. It hadn't been slept in. Zeke's stomach fluttered, but it had nothing to do with last night's drinking.

Pierre, a stocky Haitian with drowsy eyes nodded as he shuffled by. Zeke grabbed his shoulder.

"Hey, did you see Josué leave this morning?

Pierre yawned as he glanced at Josué's bunk.

"No," he grunted.

"Did you see him come in?"

Pierre looked at Zeke with an annoyed expression.

"Do I look like his mama?"

He snatched his shoulder away then continued to the latrine. Zeke stared at his friend's bed. Maybe he spent the night with his friends. Zeke remembered the faces of the man and woman who Josué left with. Although they looked as though they knew his friend, they did not look friendly.

Zeke shrugged; he would investigate it later. For now, he needed to get in uniform and get his things in order. In three days, they mustered out, leaving the arid climate of España Nueva's Arizona Territory, and returning to the vibrant dampness of New Orleans.

He shaved then dressed. At 0800 the commander, the immaculate Capitiane Loubens Saint Fleur, strode into the room as the men stood at attention before their bunks. Zeke marveled at how the man was always perfectly dressed. Even his thick, waxed mustache seemed starched and pressed like his uniform. The creole capitaine strolled down the ranks, inspecting each soldier with his keen eye. Despite the end of the campaign, the meticulous commander still demanded rigid discipline and dress, which was another thing Zeke wouldn't miss when he mustered out. The capitaine was particularly fond of harassing Zeke.

Saint Fleur halted before Zeke, giving him his special attention. He scrutinized him from head to toe, kneeling to inspect his books then rising slowly as he stared. Their faces finally met, and the capitaine frowned.

"You smell terrible, Freedonian," he said.

Zeke smiled. "It was a good night, monsieur."

The capitaine's frown deepened. "Despite that your uniform is passable. We'll make a Haitian out of you yet."

"I hope not monsieur," Zeke snapped. "My mama might not recognize me."

The capitaine smirked. "I would have kicked you out of this army long ago if you weren't such a good shot."

He glanced to Josué's bunk.

"Where is your comrade?"

Zeke's expression became serious as his stomach tightened.

"I don't know, monsieur."

Saint Fleur's eyes narrowed.

"We'll discuss this later in my office," he said.

"Yes, monsieur," Zeke replied. He was about to suffer another reprimand. Saint Fleur paired all the soldiers in his unit. Each was responsible for the other, both were rewarded and punished equally. Just another reason for Zeke to be upset with Josué.

"Comrades," the capitaine said, "we muster out in two days. New Haiti thanks you for your valiant service. Most of you will remain a part of our glorious army, although many of you will move on to new lives or return to old ones. For those of you leaving, I express my deepest sympathy."

The soldiers laughed. The capitaine did not.

"Take this time to make sure your equipment is secure and handle any business you have with the local population. The airships will arrive in El Mirage at 1200 Thursday morning. You will be in formation on the landing field by 1130. Do you understand?"

"Yes, monsieur!" the soldiers responded.

"Bon. Continue your duties. Culpepper, come with me."

The capitaine strode from the room. Zeke shrugged his shoulders, then followed. The capitaine's office was as perfect as his uniform, the walls festooned with awards and accolades. He sat behind his desk then motioned for Zeke to sit in the chair on the opposite side.

"I'm giving you the day to find Josué," he said. "Can you do that without getting into trouble?"

"I can, monsieur."

"Bon. I'm assuming that he must have some local obligations he's handling."

'Local obligation' was the commander's phrase for a girlfriend or family. The Grand Army had served in Arizona for three years, so it was only natural that some of the men developed relationships with the local women. The problem was a few had families in New Haiti. Josué was one of those few.

"I don't think it has anything to do with that," Zeke replied. "Last time I saw him he was leaving the saloon with a fancy dressed man and woman."

Saint Fleur held up his hand. "Please. I don't need to know the details. Just bring him back."

"Yes, monsieur."

Zeke stood to leave.

"Culpepper, this errand does not relieve you of your other duties. I expect you to complete them as well before Thursday."

"Of course, monsieur."

The commander began studying papers on his desk.

"You're dismissed."

Zeke saluted then exited the office.

"Asshole," he whispered.

Zeke hurried to the stables, secured a horse then rode to Luna Oscura. Few citizens walked the dusty streets; most were tending their farms in the nearby fertile valley or working the railroad. He hitched his horse then strolled through the swinging doors. The saloon was deserted except for the escort bartender. It was an American model; big, bulky and spewing steam from its head pipe like a mini locomotive.

"Hola," it said in a shrill voice. "¿Cómo puedo servirte?"

Zeke frowned. His French was passable, but his Spanish was terrible.

"Yo no hablo español," he replied.

A red light blinked near its head pipe and the escort rolled into the back. Moments later the bleary-eyed bartender from the night before came to the bar.

"Comment puis-je vous aider?" the bartender said.

"I'd prefer speaking in English if you know it," Zeke replied.

"I do."

"Do you remember me from last night?"

"I do," the bartender said. "You're the man who drank himself sick."

"How did you know I got sick?" Zeke asked.

"I've been a bartender a long time," he replied. "I know when a person is about to puke. It's how I keep my floors clean."

"Do you remember the man I came in with?"

"Josué? Of course. One of my best customers. Spends too much time in here if you ask me."

Zeke couldn't argue with him about that. He stuck out his hand and they shook.

"What's your name?" Zeke asked.

"Rodrigo," the man replied.

"Nice to meet you, Rodrigo. I'm Zeke. Look Rodrigo, I got a dilemma. You see, my friend didn't come back to the barracks last night. Last I saw, he left with a fancy dressed man and woman. I tried to go with him, but he told me not to worry. I wish I hadn't listened to him. But it's too late now. My commander sent me to find him, and I was hoping you could help me."

Rodrigo's face paled.

"Listen to me mister," he said. "If your friend left with those two, he is in serious trouble."

"Who are they and where would they take him?" Zeke asked.

Rodrigo swallowed. "I can't say. All I can tell you is that you should go back to your barracks and tell your commander that your friend is dead."

Zeke felt a chill in his gut, Rodrigo's last words knocking whatever dregs of inebriation out of him.

"What do you mean, dead?"

Rodrigo looked away as he pretended to clean glasses.

"That's all I can say, Zeke. To share anymore would put my life in jeopardy and I'm not about to die for a Haitian soldier. I have a family, too."

"I'm not leaving until you tell me who those damn people were!"

"I tell you and we're both as dead as your friend," Rodrigo replied.

"Look, I know you don't know me very well, but you don't want to be on my bad side."

Rodrigo reached under the bar then pulled out a double-barreled shotgun.

"I told you . . ."

Zeke snatched the gun from Rodrigo's hands before he could finish his sentence. The escort rolled into the barroom. Zeke spun then fired one barrel into the automaton's headpiece, sending it rolling back into the back room. He turned back to Rodrigo.

"This wasn't what I planned, but you made the first move," Zeke said. "Is there anybody in this town willing to tell me anything?"

"Go to the mining camp," Rodrigo said. "You may find someone stupid enough to talk to you there. But you'll have to pay for it."

Zeke tipped his hat. "Much obliged to you. Sorry things had to turn out this way. No hard feelings."

Rodrigo answered Zeke with a scowl.

Zeke didn't take any chances. He backed out the door then unloaded the shotgun, placing the extra shell in his pocket then throwing the gun as far as he could. He unhitched his horse then galloped out of town back to the base. Zeke jumped off his horse before the barracks and ran to the capitaine's office. Saint Fleur looked up from his papers, startled.

"Culpepper, what is the meaning for this intrusion?" he snapped.

"Sorry monsieur, but it looks like we got a situation on our hands."

"Explain," Saint Fleur said.

"Looks like them folks Josué left with are some bad people," Zeke replied. "The bartender said if Josué left with them he's probably dead."

Saint Fleur placed down his pen then steepled his fingers.

"This is a grave development," he said. He looked at Zeke, his eyes serious.

"How much time do you need?" he asked.

"Two days at least," Zeke replied. "Honestly, I don't know how long it might take. The bartender wasn't exactly giving away information, and I suspect nobody else will either."

"I won't leave one of my men in this place," the commander said. "Take all the time you need. Bring Josué back, Culpepper. Bring him back alive . . . or dead."

"I'm counting on alive," Zeke said. "If it's okay with you I think I need to do this out of uniform. I might have to do some things that wouldn't reflect too kindly on the Grand Army."

"Of course," the commander said. "Do what you need to do and take whatever you need."

"Merci, monsieur," Zeke said.

"God's speed," Saint Fleur replied.

"You might want to keep God out of this," Zeke replied. "Things might get ugly."

* * *

The miners' camp was a days' ride from town. It lay at the end of a dirt road that wound through rocky peaks and ended in a formerly wooded valley sliced by the Pecos River. The valley had once been a haven for the local wildlife, but once gold was found in the river ten years ago the unspoiled landscape was swamped by folks hoping to find an instant fortune in the once crystal waters. The trees were cut to provide shanties and the animals hunted almost to oblivion to provide food for the hungry settlers. Once the gold was depleted from the now muddy river, miners bored into the hills seeking rich gold veins within the rock. Those in search of easy wealth dwindled, while those with fewer prospects remained to work in the mines. They labored not for the fortune they once sought, but for the stability of steady work and a meager paycheck.

Zeke looked down into the town from atop a bare hill. The town sprawled along the riverbank, smoke rising from the chimneys of the small homes and businesses scattered on both sides. Somewhere down there was a person that could tell him where to find Josué. With no idea where to start, he would go to the best place to begin, the saloon.

"Let's go," he said as he reined his horse. The mare tipped down the hill, followed by the mule carrying his provisions. Fifteen minutes later he traveled down the dusty main street. The town was mostly empty, the residents most likely making their time in the mines. The saloon was easy to find, its entrance crowned with a wooden sign, the words 'Paradise' barely visible through the grime. The hints of better days could be seen in the fancy columns and windows; the swing door was made of rich mahogany wood. Zeke hitched the mare and mule then walked inside. The saloon was deserted; there was no one tending bar.

"Anybody home?" he called out from the doorway.

He heard a door open upstairs and the sound of hard shoes hitting wooden planks. A woman appeared at the top of the stairs wearing a simple white blouse and a blue cotton skirt that fell to her ankles. Her auburn hair was pulled up into a bun. She had a pretty yet hard look about her.

"We're closed," she said in a husky voice. "Come back at 5:00 pm."

"I'm not here for service, ma'am," Zeke replied. "I'm here for information."

The woman folded her arms across her chest. "What kind of information?"

"I'm looking for a friend," he said. "Last time I saw him was two days ago. He was with a couple of fancy folks before he disappeared."

The woman laughed. "You ain't gonna find anybody fancy here. We're mining folks."

"What about the folks who own the mines?" Zeke asked.

A flash of anger appeared on the woman's face. She stomped down the stairs to the bar.

"Come on in, mister," she said. "Let's have a drink."

Zeke met the woman at the bar. They shook hands; her grip was strong, her hands calloused.

"Name's Diana," she said.

"Zeke."

"Good to meet you, Zeke. What's your poison?"

"Whiskey, straight."

Diana smirked. "My kind of man. I like 'em brown and strong."

Diana winked then grabbed the whiskey bottle from the shelf with one hand and two shot glasses with the other. She filled the glasses and they both drank. Diana wiped her mouth with the back of her hand as she placed her glass on the bar.

"The Duvals own this mine and every inch of the land between here and those hills," she said. "They're the closest thing to twin devils walking God's green earth."

"Duval doesn't sound Spanish," Zeke commented.

"It ain't," Diana replied. "They're Americans just like me, although I hate to claim them. I came during the first gold rush. Made enough money to buy this saloon. They showed up just about when the gold began to peter out. Offered decent money for everybody's claims and good jobs for those willing to stay and work the mine they planned on building. They built that mine, but everything else was a goddamn lie."

Zeke held his glass out for another shot of whiskey. Diana obliged.

"These Duvalls. What do they look like?" Zeke asked.

"Couldn't tell them from the locals, especially how they dress. You'd think they was Spaniards."

Zeke nodded his head.

"It was them alright," he replied. "But I don't understand why they would show up to do something they could pay somebody to do."

Diana sucked her teeth. "If the Duvals show up on your doorstep, then you're in deep shit. Your friend must have owed them a lot of pesos."

"The bartender in El Mirage was afraid to talk about them," Zeke said. "You don't seem to have a problem."

"They can't do anything to me they already haven't," Diana replied.

"Why don't you just leave?"

"Wish it was that easy," Diana said. "I owe them, and when you owe the Duvals, you just don't walk away."

"So where do I find them?"

Diana drank another shot.

"Follow the river south about five miles. You'll come to a ford and a road that heads due east. Stay on that road for another five miles until you see the mission. That's where they'll be."

"They live in a mission?"

"That ain't no mission no more. It's a goddamn fortress. The graveyard? It's filled with folks that owed them money and didn't pay. There are rumors that the Duvals ain't right, that they do things to people before they kill 'em. Things that make death a blessing."

"Thanks for the information," Zeke said. "Looks like I need to pay the Duvals a visit."

Diana eyes bucked. "You're going by yourself?"

"Yes I am."

"I thought you was going back and bringing the Grand Army! That's the only reason I told you what I did."

"Nope," Zeke said. "I'm handling this alone."

"Shit," Diana said. "We're good as dead then."

"We'll see about that," Zeke said. He finished his whiskey then headed for his horses.

"Wait a minute!"

Diana climbed over the bar as Zeke turned about. She threw her arms around his shoulders then kissed him hard. He inhaled stale breath and whiskey before he finally pushed Diana away. She smiled as if she had found a gold nugget.

"Might as well get one now," she said. "Since you won't be coming back. Like I said, I like 'em brown and strong. And I never kissed a dead man before."

Zeke scowled. "Thanks for the vote of confidence."

Zeke pushed through the door and went to his horses. Diana followed him outside.

"Hey Zeke," Diana shouted. "Just in case you do survive, you know where to find me!"

Zeke chuckled as he mounted his horse.

"I won't be looking, that's for damn sure."

As Zeke rode for the outskirts of town a steam whistle blew, signaling the end of the morning shift. He looked toward the shaft openings and witnessed a grim sight. Armed guards were the first to emerged, hulking men holding Winchesters wearing khaki uniforms and wide brim hats. The workers trudged out moments later. They were dirty and frail, their eyes emitting the hopelessness conveyed by their appearance. Most of them didn't look strong enough to make it to the hills, let alone climb them. Anger stirred in his gut as he watched the sad procession, making him wish that he had come with the Grand Army, if only to free these desperate folks from what was slavery disguised as work. But the Army's campaign was done in España Nueva; a treaty had been signed between the rival nations bringing hostilities to an end for the moment. Zeke noticed the guards looking in his direction, so he kicked his horse and hurried from the town. He wasn't running from a fight; he just didn't have time for one. He had to find Josué.

At sundown he set up camp three miles away from the town near a clump of trees on the banks of the Pecos. Zeke sat before his fire, chewing on salt pork and sipping coffee. He figured he'd get as close to the Duvals' mission as he dared to study the building. It was most likely heavily guarded, but on the other hand the Duvals might be so confident in their control that they didn't pay attention to such details. Still, it would do him good to be cautious. He felt guilty taking a rest; every moment not

looking for Josué increased the chances that he
would never find his friend dead or alive. But he
wouldn't be any good to anyone if he was tired, so
he had to rest. He finished his meal, put out the fire
then set up a place to sleep within the trees. First
thing in the morning he would set out on foot to the
mission.

It was the mule that woke him. The agitated
beast braying alarmed Zeke. At first, he thought it
might be under attack by a puma or coyotes, but the
voices he heard soon afterwards revealed the source
of its annoyance. Zeke rolled onto his stomach,
grabbing his Henri. Looking toward the sound, he
spotted the light of three torches near the river. He
placed the Henri down then picked up the machete.
If shots were fired, he had no doubt the sound
would carry to the mission, and he would have a lot
more trouble to handle. This would have to be wet
work. Three men would be tough, but he had no
choice.

Zeke rustled about loud enough for the men
to hear then scampered away from his position. He
watched the men creep toward the woods and heard
the click of revolver hammers being locked into
place.

"We don't know who the hell you are," a gruff
voice called out. "But you're on private property.
Best you come on out now before things get ugly."

Zeke responded by tossing a stick to where
he'd slept. As soon as the stick hit a tree the men

rushed into the woods. Zeke scurried as well; his footfalls masked by the interlopers' movements.

"He's not..."

Zeke slammed his machete hilt into the man's head before he could finish his words. The man crumpled to the ground as Zeke leapt over him, slamming into the other two with his shoulder. One man, fell and Zeke kicked him across the jaw, knocking him unconscious. The third man was raising his gun when Zeke chopped down on his wrist. There was a clanging sound; the man's arm dropped but his hand was still intact.

The man grinned as he raised his gun to fire. Zeke sidestepped then grabbed the revolver with his free hand. He snatched the gun away then struck the man hard across the jaw. To his dismay the man swiveled in a circle at his waist, striking Zeke across the jaw with a backhand. Zeke fell against a nearby tree and barely avoided a punch that split the tree in half. Zeke ducked and dodged the man-thing's onslaught, looking for the right moment to strike. He stopped before a thick tree, feigning exhaustion. The man grinned as he swung at Zeke with a knife hand. Zeke ducked then watched the hand lodged into the thick tree trunk. The man grimaced as he tried to jerk his hand free. Zeke swung his machete and cut off the man's head. The sound of hissing filled the trees, the man's body collapsing to the ground as steam whooshed from its neck.

"I'll be damned," Zeke whispered. He'd seen advanced escorts before, but nothing like this.

Whoever created it managed to merge man and machine. Everything below the man's neck was mechanized metal. A sick realization came to him as he tied up the unconscious men then broke camp. He had to reach the mission as soon as possible. Despite his better judgment he worked his way up the road in darkness, urgency overruling common sense. Providence was on his side as he reached a steep rise in the trail. Zeke left the mule at the base of the hill then led the horse to the crescent. He hunkered down when he saw the torchlight below. He assumed it came from the mission, but he wouldn't be sure until daybreak. With nothing left to do, he secured the horse then attempted to rest until daybreak.

He was wide awake as the sun eased over the horizon, painting the sky with reddish hues. The light revealed the land below him and a grim smile creased his face. Zeke stared down from the hilltop at the Duval mission. He took out his spyglass for a closer look. The building sat out in the open surrounded by scrub grass and cactus, its stucco walls matching the surrounding sand. A cemetery occupied the ground before the entrance. Most of the tombstones were withered from age, but a good number were recent.

There was no way he could approach the old building without being seen. He spotted two guards. One guard patrolled the grounds, occasionally stopping to take a pull from his cigar. The other leaned against the adobe wall on the second floor. Neither seemed diligent; they worked for the Duvals, and according to the bartender no one in their right mind would dare attack their stronghold. But Zeke wasn't in his right mind.

He folded his spyglass then tucked it in his pocket before crawling behind the summit. His horse munched on a clump of grass, oblivious to the role it was about to play. Zeke did a self-inspection one last time. He wore a Colt on each hip, his waist belt rimmed with bullets. Two ammo belts of shotgun shells crisscrossed his chest. His shotgun rested in his leg holster and his machete in its sheath across his back. Strapped to his right calf was a dagger; on his left calf was his Derringer. He sauntered to his horse then took his Henri from the saddle holster. He had the least number of rounds for it but didn't plan on using the rifle once he got inside the mission. If he reached the mission.

"Got dammit Josué," he said. "Damn you to hell!"

Zeke took the whiskey flask from his saddle, twisted off the cap then drank it dry, wiping his mouth as the liquor burned its way to his stomach. He considered walking away, but he'd come too far. He couldn't leave a friend behind, especially if he knew what would happen if he did.

Zeke grabbed the horse's reins then led it to the hillcrest. He slapped the horse's flank as hard as he could. The horse whinnied then bolted over the hill toward the mission. Zeke darted to his right, keeping as low as he could and praying that the horse would keep the guards distracted until he was close. If he could make it to the cemetery before they saw him, he'd have some kind of cover once the shooting started. But that wasn't to be. A shot

rang out; Zeke heard the bullet buzz past his head.
Thank God for bad shots, he thought. He lifted his
Henri, working the lever furiously as he gunned the
man down, the extra shots just in case the man was
an automaton. He wasn't. Bullets streaked by him
and peppered the dirt around his feet as he dodged
through the tombstones. A bullet grazed his shoulder as he reached the walls, spinning him around.
Zeke would have fallen if not being so close to the
wall. He grimaced as he slammed against it, his
hand going to the wound. He bled, but the wound
was superficial.

He gathered himself then edged toward the
gate. As he expected the wooden barrier swung
wide, unleashed a half dozen guards. Zeke am-
bushed them, killing all six in a matter of seconds.
He ran to the door, entering the mission sanctuary.
He ducked behind the closest pew as more guards
released a storm of gunfire. Zeke dropped the Henri
then snatched the revolvers from his holsters. He'd
be stupid to try to work his way through such a barrage, so he would wait for them to come to him.

And come they did. The first guard leapt over
the pew, guns blazing. Zeke rolled away and fired
back, striking the man in the torso. Zeke burst from
cover, sprinting up the left side of the pews, shooting every step of the way. His goal was the doors behind the altar. Luck and speed got him to the closed
door on the right. To his chagrin it was locked. He
kicked near the lock, but the door refused to give.
Zeke holstered his revolver then snatched out his
shotgun and blasted the lock away. He kicked the
door again and it flew open, revealing a long corri-
dor with rooms on either side.

Zeke ducked into the first room. A stench as-
sailed his nose; he looked about and nearly

vomited. The room was filled with rotting body parts, legs and limbs strewn over tables and benches. He fled the room, barreling into the guards that pursued him. A close quarter melee ensued, guns firing and fists and knife blades flying. It was over in moments, with Zeke staggering wounded down the hallway, leaving a pile of dead and wounded men behind him.

"Josué!" he shouted. "Where the hell are you?"

"Zeke!" Josué shouted back.

Zeke sprinted into the room from which Josué's voice emanated. As he charged through the door he stumbled to a stop. Josué, or what was left of him, sat on a bare table. His body was gone, replaced by a metal assembly like the guard he'd killed the night before. He heard a sound behind him and spun, his shotgun raised. Two figures stood in the doorway draped in white coats, their faces covered by surgical masks. Both pointed revolvers at Zeke. They removed their masks, revealing the man and woman Zeke assumed were the Duvals.

The man snarled as he spoke.

"You are a dead man," he said. "You'll never leave this building alive."

"Never," the woman said.

"You first," Zeke answered.

He blasted the man and woman into the hallway before they could fire. He lowered the shotgun then turned to Josué.

"Zeke," Josué said, tears streaming from his eyes. "Do it."

"Do what?" Zeke replied.

"Kill me, Zeke. I can't live like this. I can't."

Zeke's hands trembled.

"I . . . can't," he replied.

"Look at me, mon frere," Josué whispered. "I can't go back to my family like this. I'm a monster."

Zeke shook his head. "No. No."

"Then let me do it," Josué said. "Give me a revolver."

Zeke didn't reply.

"Please Zeke. Please."

Zeke took a revolver from his holster then sat it by Josué's metal hand.

"Merci, mon ami," he said. "Merci."

"Goodbye, brother," Zeke replied.

He turned his back and hurried from the room. Zeke was halfway down the hall when the gun fired. He stopped for a moment, closing his eyes and whispering a prayer before continuing. Darkness settled inside him, a blackness that covered his heart and infected his thoughts. He reloaded his guns then walked from room to room, hunting for any person in the mission. Those he found alive he killed; those that were dead he put another bullet in them for good measure. When he was done, he sought and found the storage room. There were two canisters of kerosene; he emptied the contents throughout the building. He exited the structure, lit a match then tossed it inside. He waited for the fire to catch before closing the doors then trudging away. By the time he reached the hilltop the mission was fully ablaze.

* * *

Zeke arrived at the base mid-afternoon, two days after his encounter at the mission. His comrades looked at him warily his horse and mule sauntered by. He entered the fort then made his way to the commander's office. He secured his beasts and entered the headquarters. Saint Fleur looked up to Zeke's grim face and frowned.

"I'm sorry," he said.

Zeke plopped into the chair before the commander's desk and took off his hat.

"Did you bring back his body?" Saint Fleur asked.

"Wasn't much to bring back," Zeke answered.

Zeke told Saint Fleur everything. The commander's face reflected his horror and revulsion.

"You did the right thing," he said as Zeke finished. "I'll write a letter to his family. We'll say it was combat related. Best to spare them the details."

"That's kind of you, sir," Zeke replied. "If you don't mind, I'd like to deliver that letter. It's the least I can do."

"Of course," the commander replied. "Like I said, you are a good man, Zeke Culpepper. If you ever decide to come to your senses and rejoin the Grand Army, I'd be happy to serve as your commander."

"Thank you, sir, but that won't happen," Zeke replied. "I'm done with killing. Think I'll go back home and try my luck at farming."

"I don't see you as a farmer," Saint Fleur said.

"I don't either," Zeke confessed. "But there's a farm waiting for me in Georgia, so I might as well give it a try."

The commander nodded.

"Gather your gear. We leave within the hour."

Zeke returned to his bunk. He stripped out of his civvies then took a long shower, all the while trying to shake the image of Josué sitting on the white table, more machine than man. He returned to his bunk then donned his uniform as the other soldiers left the room for the airship field. Zeke glanced at Josué's empty bunk, and the grief hit him all at once. He sat hard on his bed then covered his face with his hands, hiding the tears escaping his eyes despite his best effort.

"God damn it Josué!" he shouted. "God damn it!"

He let the tears flow for a few minutes more before wiping his face and straightening his uniform. Zeke threw his duffel bag over his left shoulder, his weapon case across his back then strode to the field. The airships had arrived, the armored dirigibles completing their final landing approach. As the crafts eased down to the field, Zeke managed to smile as he remembered his friend. Josué was the last person that would want him to brood over his death. He'd done what his friend asked him to do. Josué was at peace. In the end, that was all that mattered.

Home

The Night of Lights celebration began at sundown in the Summerhill District and Synthia was almost ready. She checked her makeup one last time then ran her hand over her bald scalp. Stubble scratched her palms; she would need to shave soon. She summoned her holoscreen to confirm her sources were fully charged. Satisfied, she waved away the screen, exited her twenty-first-floor condo and strode to the lift. Synthia pressed the door button and moments later was greeted by the friendly faces of other celebrants from the upper floors, all dressed in the traditional black robe with high collars bordering their exuberant faces. No words were shared; no one wanted to spoil the energy with words.

The lift door opened, and Synthia and the other riders flowed into the condo lobby then out into the lighted streets. The crisp air chilled her brown skin and she grinned. Fall was her favorite time of year. Bradford Pear trees and sugar maples blazed autumn orange, adding to the festive atmosphere. Synthia blinked and her eyes turned yellow, matching the hue radiated by the inside of her robe. The others around her did the same, surrounding her with reds, blues, greens, and all the colors of the spectrum. While the others paired off, Synthia strolled the leaf littered streets alone. She was new to the neighborhood and had yet to make friends. It was just a matter of time. There were only so many of them in Atlanta, and there was safety in numbers.

"Synthia?"

She turned and her eyebrows rose. Bryan, her brother, forced a smile on his face as he approached.

"I thought that was you," he said. "You've changed . . ."

"Everything," she finished for him. "What are you doing here? I thought you hated synths."

"I do . . . I mean I don't, at least not you. You're not a synth."

"I am, Bryan."

"No, you're not!" Bryan blurted. "Not inside. You're my sister."

Synthia placed her hand on her younger brother's shoulder then smiled when he flinched.

"Who sent you?" she asked. "I know you didn't come on your own. And who told you how to find me? Mama?"

"Yes."

"So why are you here?"

Bryan's eyes glistened. "It's daddy. He's dying. He asked for you. But . . ."

"But what?"

Synthia waited for Bryan to answer.

"I don't think he'll want to see you like this."

"Is that what daddy thinks, or you?"

Bryan shrugged.

"I don't know. I'm just the messenger," Bryan said. "Do what you want."

"I'll think about it."

Bryan shoved his hands into his pockets and pulled in his shoulders.

"Fine." He marched away.

"Don't think too long," he called out. "He doesn't have much time. Not all of us choose to live forever."

Synthia watched him walk away. She should just let him go and be done with it, but she couldn't. Mama didn't send him to Aytee-El for them to fight. She could have texted.

"Bryan, wait."

She trotted up to him then grabbed his arm.

"How did you get here?" she asked.

"I took the bullet from Valdosta," he replied without turning.

"You must be hungry. Tired, too."

Bryan turned his head just enough for her to see the side of his face.

"I am. Hungry, that is."

"Come with me," she said as she tugged his arm.

"Where are you taking me?"

"To my favorite restaurant."

He turned to face her.

"You still eat food? Real food?"

Synthia laughed at his ignorant question.

"Yes, I do. Now come on."

She tried to take his hand, but he pulled away. She started to say something sarcastic but decided not to. They were inseparable growing up, only two years apart. Time and circumstances change everything, some more than others.

They weaved through the growing crowd of lighted revelers. Bryan was making a huge effort not to bump into anyone. His noticeable avoidance drew laughs and scowls from passersby.

Synthia was relieved when they finally reached Shay's Ramen Shack.

"Let's eat outside,' she said. "It's such a pleasant night."

Bryan followed her to an empty table. A server appeared seconds later, his voluminous afro strobing from red, to black, to green then back to red.

"Hey, Synthia!" he said. "Who's your friend?"

"Tay, meet Bryan, my baby brother. Bryan, Tay."

Bryan struggled to smile. "Nice to meeting you, Tay."

"Same here," Tay replied. "So, what'll you and the normal have?"

"Come on Tay, be nice," Synthia said. "He's my brother."

Tay winked. "Alright alright. Just teasing. What'll you have, baby doll?"

"The usual," Synthia replied. "Bryan?"

Bryan squinted as he read the menu. "I have no idea. I've never had ramen before."

Tay stood beside Bryan, and Synthia dropped and shook her head when Bryan leaned away.

"You like spicy?" Tay asked.

"A little," Bryan replied.

"Let's start you off with the Dan Dan Man-zeman," he said. "I guess since you're a South Georgia boy you ain't afraid of pork."

Bryan grinned. "From the rooter to the tooter."

Tay laughed and his hair color sequence quickened. Bryan's mouth fell open.

"I know, right?" Tay said. "It gets everybody."

Tay took their menus.

"I'll be back with water and edamame."

Bryan stared at Tay until he entered the restaurant.

"This is crazy," he said.

"You get used to it," Synthia replied. "I had to adjust. It's nothing like home."

"You can say that again," Bryan agreed. "Why would he do that?"

Synthia shrugged. "Why not? If you're buying a new model, you might as well go all out."

"You didn't."

"I'm from South Georgia," Synthia replied. "Old habits are hard to break."

"And I didn't like the way he called me normal."

Synthia tilted her head. "Kinda like the way you say synth?"

Bryan looked away, embarrassed.

"He was teasing you," Synthia explained. "Tay is good people, but he never misses a chance to take a jab at a normal, even if it's my brother."

Tay returned with their waters and a bowl of edamame. Synthia took one of the salted soybeans then popped it into her mouth. Bryan took one from the bowl then studied it before he did the same.

"This is good," he said.

"Yep," Synthia replied.

"Is this real food," Bryan asked.

"No, it's synthetic."

Bryan grabbed his throat and Synthia laughed.

"It's real," she said. "You'll be shitting it out in a few hours."

"Your sense of humor hasn't changed," Bryan said.

"Why should it?"

Bryan ate more edamame. "I don't know."

Synthia reached out and took his hand. This time he didn't pull away.

"It's the same me, Bryan. Nothing's change."

Bryan folded his arms as he leaned back in his chair.

"Well, nothing important," she finished.

Bryan was opening mouth to reply when Tay appeared with their bowls. He placed Synthia 's down first, then gave Bryan his.

"Thank you," Bryan said.

"I love Southern folks," Tay said. "So polite. Now eat up."

Bryan scooped up a spoonful then ate.

"Wow. This is delicious!" he said with a full mouth.

"My job is done here," Tay said. He winked at Synthia. "Enjoy!"

Synthia began eating her ramen.

"Is he synth?" Bryan asked.

"We all are," Synthia replied.

"No, I mean is he one hundred percent synth?"

"Does it matter?"

Bryan fell silent. Synthia watched him eat, expecting him to continue.

"I guess it doesn't matter here," he finally said.

"It doesn't matter anywhere, except in South Georgia."

"There are other places," Bryan said.

"The list gets shorter every day," Synthia said. "Japan is 85% synth. China's not far behind. Europe's up to 40%, and Africa and South America are around 50%."

"What about Atlanta?" Bryan asked.

"Around 40%," Synthia answered. She picked up her bowl then slurped down the remaining broth.

"Hurry up and finish," she said. "I got a great pastry shop I want to take you."

Bryan finished his ramen. Tay came, took their bowls then scanned Synthia's wrist for payment.

The crowd was thick, synths and normals mingled together enjoying the revelry. Synthia could sense Bryan's mood easing and it made her smile. She was still big sister, looking out for baby brother. They got separated for a few minutes; when she found him a cute petite woman with glowing turquoise eyes that matched her robe lights had him pinned against the wall, talking so fast she didn't give him any time to reply.

"There you are, sweetheart!" she exclaimed. She grabbed his hand then dragged him away, the woman scowling at her as she waved.

"Thank you!" Bryan said.

"You're welcome," Synthia replied. "Although she was kinda cute."

Bryan looked embarrassed. "Yes, she was. Except for her eyes. They were creepy."

"You mean like this?"

Synthia's eyes went from subtle to glaring yellow. Bryan shaded his face.

"Stop that, please!"

Synthia almost laughed until she detected the tone of his voice. He was terrified.

The sound of bongos and bass broke the tension. Synthia grabbed Bryan's hand.

"Come on! It's starting!"

The entire crowd surged in the same direction, the music louder as they neared the outdoor stage. The band was deep into an amapiano vibe, their holoimages flanking their performance. Synthia and Bryan pushed their way close to the stage. Synthia warmed inside when she saw the genuine smile on her brother's face.

"Come on," she said. "Let's show them how the Robinsons get down!"

There were two things Bryan and Synthia loved more than anything else: music and dancing. They cleared space with their flamboyant moves, drawing an audience that began cheering them on. Other dancers joined them and soon it was a true celebration. They danced until the band and DJ gave up the stage to a jazz trio.

"I haven't danced like that in a long time," Bryan said as they sauntered away from the outdoor stadium.

"I don't believe that," Synthia said. "Not Mr. Partyman himself."

"Hasn't been much partying in Moultrie," Bryan replied. "Everyone is preparing for Transition."

"I can imagine," Synthia said. She glanced up to the near invisible dome that covered Aytee-El. The United Cities passed the Human Separation Act thirty years ago and construction of the megacity domes began immediately afterwards. Now that the cities and the domes were also most complete, the hard part was beginning. Synthia's life wouldn't change much; she'd been living in Aytee-El for three years and her lifestyle fit the new normal. But it would be hard for people like Bryan and the other members of her family.

"Are y'all coming to Aytee-El?" she asked.

"No. Jayville," Bryan replied. "It's closer, plus it's near the ocean. You know how I love the beach."

'Beach access will be restricted. You know that, right?"

"Yeah, I know," Bryan said. "But at least I'll be able to look at it."

Synthia hooked her arm around Bryan's.

"You're staying with me tonight," she said.

"I don't think that's a good idea. I need to get back to mama and daddy."

"Call mama," she said. "Let me talk to her."

Bryan took out his phone.

"Mama . . . How's daddy . . . Yes, I found her. She wants to speak to you."

Bryan extended the phone to Synthia. She hesitated before taking it.

"Hey mama."

"Oh Lordy! Hey baby!"

The tears came before she could stop them.

"I'm sorry I haven't called."

"It's alright Cyndy. We're talking now."

"Bryan's going to spend the night with me. Is that okay?"

"Of course! Me and your daddy will be fine."

Synthia moved the phone closer to her mouth. "Can I talk to daddy?"

"He's asleep. Why don't you give him a call tomorrow? I know he'd love to speak to you."

"Okay mama, I will. Bye. Love you."

"Love you, too, sweety."

Synthia gave the phone back to Bryan.

"You heard mama. You're spending the night with me."

"I'm a grown ass man," Bryan said.

"Who's spending the night with his big sister," Synthia replied.

Bryan looked like he was trying to keep a bee in his mouth when a smile finally burst on his face.

"Good! Now that that's settled, let's go get a Juicy Pop."

"Juicy Pop?"

"Only the best popsicle known to humankind."

Synthia grabbed his hand, and they ran toward the restaurant district.

* * *

Synthia 's apartment occupied a corner on the 14th floor of a complex overlooking Hank Aaron Boulevard. She sat at her balcony table, sipping rum and seltzer water while gazing at the construction drones working on the final phase of the dome. In a few more years humans would cut themselves off from Mother Earth in hopes that She would be able to heal without their presence. It was a first; the first time a virus quarantined itself from its host.

The glass door slid open, and Bryan stepped out. He grinned then sat at the table.

"What you looking at?"

Synthia pointed into the sky.

"It's really happening," he said.

"Yep."

"Doesn't seem right," he said.

"It doesn't matter," Synthia said. "It's happening."

They were silent for a moment before Bryant spoke again.

"Why did you do it?" he asked.

"Do what?" Synthia asked, as if she didn't know.

"Change yourself?"

Synthia sighed. "Because I wanted to. And because I didn't have a choice."

"There's always a choice," Bryan replied. "At least that's what you always told me."

Synthia turned to face Bryan.

"If I tell you something, you have to promise not to tell mama and daddy."

"I promise."

Synthia swallowed then looked into the night sky.

"Five years ago, I was diagnosed with ovarian cancer," she said. Bryan sat up in his chair.

"Synthia! Why didn't you say anything?"

"I didn't want to worry anybody, especially daddy," Synthia said. "It was advanced. My doctor told me I had two options. I could fight it with radiation, but the chances were slim that I would win. Or I could do this."

She swept her hand across her body. "Both were just as risky, but if I pulled through synth transition, I'd never have to worry about cancer again."

Bryan settled back into his chair. "That wasn't much of a choice."

"Tell me about it."

Bryan sipped his drink. "I wish you would have at least told me."

"Back then you were the last person I would have told," Synthia said. "I'm still surprised you came looking for me."

"I did that for daddy," Bryan said as he looked away.

"You you're still a member of Pastor Benning's flock?"

Bryan nodded.

"Flock," she said. "That's an appropriate description."

"Don't start," Bryan warned.

Synthia rolled her eyes then took a sip of her rum seltzer.

"You could have texted. My number hasn't changed."

Bryan looked up; his eyes intense.

"My plan was to talk you into reversal," he said. "I read somewhere that a person's body was kept in cryo for three months after transition just in case the central nervous system and the synth host didn't mesh. But I see that was no option for you."

"No, it wasn't," Synthia replied. "Not that it would have made a difference."

"You saying you would have done it anyway?"

"Yeah, one day down the road," she admitted. "You still hate me?"

"I never hated you," Bryan answered. "I never could. I just didn't understand why."

"What's there to understand?" Synthia said.

"You're going to outlive us all," he said. "We're going to die, and you're going to be alone. That's not what God intended. Earth ain't Heaven."

"Who knows what God intended? I'll bet you good crypts Paster Benning doesn't. Besides, you don't think I didn't think about that?" Synthia replied. "I did. I still do. Every day."

"But I still don't . . ."

"Bryan, do you love me?" Synthia asked.

"Of course, I do," he replied.

"Then let's just go with that," Synthia said. "Let's just sit here, drink, and look at the stars."

Synthia took out her phone then turned on her playlist. Jazz wafted from her stereo on the patio and the two of them listened until they dozed off. The morning sun sent scattered beams of light between the high rises and woke them. Synthia stretched and yawned.

"You hungry?" she asked.

"Yes," Bryan replied. "What you got inside?"

"Nothing. Let's go get something then we'll catch a bullet home."

"We?"

"Yeah, I'm going with you."

Bryan's eyes widened and he smiled.

"Mama and daddy will be so happy!"

"Calm down," Synthia said. "I'm not coming for good."

Bryan's shoulders slumped.

"Oh."

"I can't. This is home now. But I'll make you a promise. I'll stay as long as daddy wants me to. Okay?"

Bryan's smile returned. "Okay."

Synthia stood. "I'm going to wash up then we'll get some grub."

"You don't need to eat, do you?" Bryan asked.

"No, but I'm going to," she said. "Can't let my baby brother pig out alone."

"You were right," Bryan said. "You are the same."

"Of course, I am," Synthia replied. "What I changed out here, didn't change who I am in here."

She placed her palm on her chest as she stood.

"Now let's freshen up and get going. Those cinnamon rolls at Big Tarts don't wait for anyone."

Bryan jumped from his chair then hurried inside. Synthia watched him go, then followed, closing the sliding door behind her.

They washed up then walked the two blocks to Big Tarts. The woman waiting on them was a normal.

"Welcome to Big Tarts," she said with a flat Midwestern accent. "What'll you have?"

"I'll have a chocolate croissant," Synthia said.

The woman turned to Bryan. "And you?"

"I'll take a cinnamon roll," he said.

A wide smile broke out on the woman's face.

"I love your accent! Where are you from?"

"South Georgia," Bryan said. "Moultrie."

"Never heard of it," she said. "Looks like they grow them big and handsome down there."

Bryan smirked. "If you say so."

"You eating here or to go?" she asked.

"To go," Synthia said.

The server picked up Synthia 's croissant with the tongs then dropped it in a small brown back with the store logo stamped on it.

"Here you go," she said.

"Thank you," Synthia said.

"You're welcome!"

She repeated the process with Bryan's cinnamon roll, but when Bryan grasped the bag with his fingers, she didn't let it go.

"My name is Heaven," she said.

"I'm Bryan," he said. "Your parents gave you an ambitious name."

"You should get to know me," Heaven said. "I live up to it."

Synthia covered her mouth to hide her grin as Bryan tugged at his bag. Heaven held onto it a little longer before letting it go."

"Thank you," he said.

"You're more than welcome. See you again soon."

"I don't think so. I'm going back home today."

"That's too bad," Heaven said.

Synthia and Bryan left the store.

"Look at you!" she said. Coming to the A and getting everybody hot and bothered."

"Leave me alone," Bryan said. "Folks up here must be desperate."

"You sure you want to move to Jayville instead of here?"

"I have to be with mama and daddy," Bryan said. "Besides, Aytee-El is too fast for a country boy like me."

"We'll all be on the same speed soon," Synthia said.

As casual as she attempted to be, Synthia worried. It was such a extreme thing, closing humanity off from the Earth. But the truth was they really had no choice. Even such a drastic decision didn't guarantee the world would heal its wounds. And even if it did, it wouldn't be in her lifetime.

They returned to her apartment, packed their items then caught a Rideout to the bullet station. The traffic was sparse; Synthia and Bryan found empty seats, with Synthia getting her favored window seat. Ten minutes after settling in, the rapid rail streaked from the A and into the agricultural sector. Every inch of ground outside the city was cultivated to supply food for the soon to be crowded metropolis. All 15 million of the state's inhabitants would soon call Aytee-El home, and the Ag sector would have to supply them with most of their food needs until the city reached full sustainable status. The same process was occurring in states, provinces, kingdoms, countries, and territories around the world. Aytee-El had been designated the population hub, expanding on the covert plans The Elites created before the Hacker War. Central Georgia was designated the agricultural sector. It was the richest soil in the state and would be used until sustainable farming was incorporated into the megacity core. Other state regions were being abandoned and given back to nature. South Georgia, Synthia 's home, was the last to transition.

The landscape changed as they entered the Coastal Plain region. They streaked by abandoned towns left to decay with pine trees emerging from sidewalk and road cracks. Buildings slowly succumbed to kudzu and muscadine vines while flocks of crows and pigeons maneuvered between abandoned buildings. Synthia glimpsed a herd of feral cows grazing on what was once Interstate I-75 and smiled. Humans weren't the only creatures in transition.

The bullet slowed then stopped at the Adele terminal, which in reality was a temporary shed large enough to protect a handful of people from the elements. No sooner did they step off the rail did Synthia begin looking about.

"Where's the Rideout?" she asked.

Bryan let out a grim laugh. "Are you serious? The UC cut off public transportation for the outliers five years ago. Another step to force us in line."

The heaviness was back in Bryan's voice. He stared at her the way he did when he saw her at the festival. To him, she was part of what was forcing them to give up their life.

"So, who's coming to pick us up?"

Bryan took out his phone then sent a text.

"Somebody will be here in a few minutes," he said.

The good vibe they shared in the Metro had been sucked away by the dismal surroundings. Every minute Synthia stood at the station reminded her why she left . . . no, fled this place. The grumble of a diesel burning truck engine broke her musing. When the dingy white Dualie came into view, Synthia felt bile rise into her mouth.

"You called him?" she said.

"He's the only person that does this," Bryan said. "Sorry. I should have said something."

The truck pulled up close and Khalid stepped out of the driver's side, his grey eyes locked on Synthia.

"Well, I'll be damn," he said. "Never thought I'd see you back here again."

Synthia didn't reply. She was too angry. She stomped to the truck, opened the passenger door then climbed inside.

"Hello to you, too," Khalid said.

Khalid and Bryan got into the truck, and they traveled to the farm, the truck bouncing and rattling over the dilapidated roads. Synthia seethed. If there was any person that could make her feel more out of place, it was Khalid.

"So how you liking Aytee-El?" he asked.

"It's fine," she replied. She looked up to see him gazing at her from the rear-view mirror.

"I see you cut off all your hair. That's a shame."

"Can we just do this quietly?" Synthia said.

Khalid grinned. "I see some things haven't changed."

Synthia let out a sigh when the family farm came into view. Bryan had done a good job maintaining it, the orderly fallow fields and freshly repaired fences resembling an invisible barrier compared to the unkempt properties surrounding it. The truck rumbled up the gravel road leading to the house. By the time they stopped mama was on the porch, her hands clasped together with a gracious smile on her brown, weathered face. Synthia 's bitterness melted away. Mama wore her favorite sweater and house dress, with a new pair of house shoes. The pickup had barely come to a stop when Synthia grabbed her bag, opened the door, and jumped out. She crunched her way to the porch, up the stairs then into mama's waiting arms.

"Hey, mama!" she said.

"Hey, baby girl."

They held each other tight for a long minute before mama's arms opened to Synthia 's disappointment. Mama stepped back then inspected her.

"At least you been eating," she said.

"You know me," Synthia said. "I ain't never missed a meal."

Mama's eyes focused on her bald scalp.

"You never did like doing your hair," she said. "Guess that's not a problem anymore."

"Nope," Synthia said.

Mama looked over Synthia 's shoulder and her smile faded.

"How you doing, Mrs. Dobson?"

Khalid stood at the steps beside Bryan. Mama's eyes narrowed.

"Hey boy," she said. "Don't you have other things to do?"

"Not right now," Khalid said, his voice expectant.

"Well, we about to spend some family time. You best be on your way. I appreciate you bring my children home."

Khalid's face drooped like a sad bloodhound. He nodded at mama then trudged back to his truck, making a ruckus spinning his tires on the gravel before speeding away.

"Never liked that boy," mama said. "I was so glad when y'all broke up."

"He broke my heart," Synthia said.

"Sometimes you need to go through a little pain for better things," mama said.

Bryan walked by them into the house.

"Mama still mama," he said.

"Come inside girl," mama said. "Your daddy been up all night waiting to see you."

Synthia entered the house and the sights and smells of her past overwhelmed her. She passed the kitchen on the way to mama and daddy's room, spotting the old pot on the gas stove, a mess of greens simmering to perfection inside. Beside it, hot oil crackled from water escaping the greens pot. Mama was cooking fried pork chops, her favorite.

They entered her parents' room. Daddy lay in the bed, the mattress raised high enough for him to see her enter. He smiled and his eyes squinted.

"There's my baby girl," he said.

"Hey, daddy!"

Synthia sat in the chair beside the bed then leaned over to hug daddy. He returned the hug with his left arm.

"I need to finish dinner," mama said.

Synthia stood. "I'll help."

"No, you won't," mama replied. "You'll stay right there with your daddy. You and I will talk later."

Synthia sat down then held daddy's hand.

"How are you feeling?"

"Terrible," Daddy replied. "But that's every day."

"I'm sorry, daddy."

"What you got to be sorry about?" Daddy said. "You ain't do nothing."

"You know what I mean," she said.

Daddy laughed until he began coughing. He pointed to the glass of water on his nightstand and Synthia gave it to him. He sipped until his coughing subsided.

"So, Bryan said you souped up."

Synthia chucked. "I'm not a car, daddy."

"You know what I'm talking about."

"I guess he told y'all everything."

"You should have."

"I didn't want y'all to worry. I'm alright now."

"Let me see."

Synthia rolled up her sleeve exposing her arm. Daddy touched her seam with his finger then traced it up to her elbow.

"I'll be damn," he said.

"You should have done it," Synthia said. Daddy shook his head.

"Too old," he said. "Body couldn't take the strain."

Synthia eyes widened in surprise.

"You talked to Dr. Cane about it?"

"Of course, I did. Checked out all the options."

"I'm surprised."

"Why?"

"Bryan said . . ."

"Since when you start listening to Bryan? He's your baby brother. That boy ain't the sharpest knife in the drawer. He takes after your mama's side."

Synthia smiled. "He looks just like you."

"The only good thing he got from me."

Daddy was teasing, which meant he was in a good mood.

"Dinner's ready!" Mama shouted. Daddy began shifting in the bed.

"Help me sit up," he said.

Synthia leaned over then wrapped her arms around daddy's torso as he hugged her neck. She lifted him to a sitting position.

"Good. Now help me stand."

Synthia drew away. "Daddy you're not supposed to . . ."

"Come on help me stand, girl," he said. "I already know you stronger than you look, and I'll be damned if I'm gonna eat in this bed with my whole family here."

Synthia wrapped her right arm around daddy's waist, and he put his left arm around her shoulders.

"Okay then," he said. "Let's make a grand entrance."

They made their way to the kitchen, daddy shuffling, Synthia supporting. Daddy was doing less than he thought, and Synthia was thankful for the bionics that helped her walk/carry her daddy to the kitchen table. Mama had her back to them, giving the greens one more stir.

"I said, dinner's ready!"

Mama dropped the lid then reached back to untie her apron.

"I swear every last one of them is deaf," she whispered.

Mama turned around as Synthia eased daddy into his chair. Her hands went to her cheeks.

"Samuel Dobson, what you done made this girl do?"

"Don't worry about it, Gurdy," daddy said.

Bryan walked into the kitchen and his eyes went wide.

"Daddy! What you doing in here?"

"I'm about to eat my dinner if y'all don't mind," he said.

Mama and Bryan glared at Synthia.

"What? He told me to do it."

Mama rolled her eyes. "Well, it's too late now. But I promise to God if you die at my table and fall face first into my red rice, I'm gonna leave you just like that until they come get you."

Daddy laughed himself into another coughing fit and Synthia ran to get him his water. Once he calmed down, she helped mama make his plate then took it to him.

"Go on sit down, mama" she said. "I'll make your plate."

"Thank you, sweetie," mama said. She sat beside daddy, and they shared a smile.

Synthia made mama's plate then her own. Bryan made his plate and joined everyone at the table. They joined hands and mama said grace. No sooner did she finish did everyone enjoy the food prepared. There was never much talking when folks sat down to eat mama's food; silence was the complement to an excellent meal. There was red rice, fried pork-chop, turnip greens and cornbread. Mama had pepper sauce and chow chow on the table; Bryan went for the sauce; mama and Synthia play fought over the chow chow. Although she enjoyed the culinary variety of the A, there was nothing like home cooking.

Daddy was the first to finish. He leaned back into his chair then rubbed his stomach.

"I swear your mama is best cook in the world!" he said. He grabbed mama's hand. "You know that's why I asked you marry me, right?"

He looked at Bryan and Synthia.

"She thought it was because she had a big booty. Used to wear the tightest jeans she could find whenever we went out."

"It was both," mama said. "You used to look at my ass like it was fried chicken."

"Oh my God stop!" Synthia said. "I don't need to hear this."

"They do this all the time," Bryan said. "At least they don't do it in public."

"Shoot, y'all grown now," daddy said. "How you think y'all got here?"

"Let's talk about something else please," Synthia said.

"Yeah, let's do that," mama said. "Let's talk about why our baby girl was about to die and decided not to tell anybody."

Synthia cut her eyes at Bryan, and he shrugged.

"They needed to know," he said.

"You should have told us," daddy said. "It would have made everything simpler."

"So, I had to be dying for y'all to handle my changes?"

"I didn't mean it like that," daddy said.

"Pastor Buckman said that which was not made by God's hands cannot enter the kingdom of Heaven," Bryan said.

"We ain't gonna talk about Buckman," mama said. "He was the first person to run off the Jayville after filling everybody up with his fool talk."

Bryan picked up his fork and picked at his greens. "I'm just saying."

"We didn't send for you to talk about things past," mama said. "We sent for you so we could talk about the future."

"You decided when you're relocating to Jayville?" Synthia asked.

"Not exactly," mama said. "We applied for a Relocation exemption."

"A what?" Bryan asked.

"Relocation exemption," Synthia said. "I heard of those, but I thought it was a joke."

"It's not," mama said. "We applied and we were approved."

"What does that mean?" Bryan said.

"It means me and your mama ain't going anywhere," daddy said. "We're staying right here."

"Yes!" Bryan said.

"Don't go celebrating, boy," mama said. "The exemption is for me and your daddy, not you."

"I thought you said 'we'," Bryan said.

"You a grown man," daddy said. "You have to make those decisions on your own."

Synthia was silent, stunned by the implications.

"Mama, Daddy. If you're here when city construction is complete, you'll be permanently cut off."

Mama and daddy held hands.

"We know," mama said.

"That means you'll be cut off from us," Synthia finished. A chill swept through her as she uttered those last words.

"What do you mean us?" Bryan said. "I'm staying, too!"

"You have to apply," Synthia said. "But I'll bet it's too late now." Her eyes narrowed.

"All this change is too much for us," Mama said. "The UC will provide us with all the support we'll need. Y'all will be notified once we move on."

Synthia 's sight blurred. She stood then stormed out the kitchen, across the porch then into the yard. She didn't stop until she reached the persimmon tree near the fallow cornfield. She took her cell from her pocket and stabbed the touchpad with her fingers. Khalid responded moments later.

Pick up?
Yes.
You just got here.
You coming or not?
On my way.

Synthia jammed the phone into her pocket then paced. She heard the screen door slam then looked up. Mama eased down the stairs then walked toward her. Synthia looked around for somewhere else to go as mama came closer.

"Nowhere else to run to, baby," mama said.

"How could you make a decision like this without talking to me and Bryan?" Synthia asked.

"We haven't seen you in two years," mama replied.

"That's not right, mama. You know how everybody treated me the last time I was home."

"We didn't treat you like that," mama said. "We've always been here for you.

Synthia felt tears on her cheek. "Just because I haven't been here doesn't mean I didn't want to be.

I always knew that if I wanted to come home, I could. But this? It's too much!"

Mama opened her arms. Synthia fell into them and sobbed.

"We can't ask you to do something you don't want to," mama said. "And you can't ask us to do something we don't want. The world is changing, and it's changing us."

"I'll stay as long as I can," Synthia whispered.

"That's good to hear, baby. Now text Khalid and cancel that ride. Dessert is getting cold. I made apple pie. Sweet potato pie, too."

Synthia looked into mama's eyes.

"I love you."

"I love you, too. Always and forever."

Synthia took mama's hand, and together they walked back to the house.

"Everybody's losing something," mama said. "It's the times. We're sacrificing for what we hope will be."

"I know," Synthia said. "It still doesn't make it better."

"We ain't gonna worry about that right now," mama said. "We got this moment, and right now you're home."

"Yes, I am," Synthia said.

Mama intertwined her arm with Synthia's.

"Let's go back inside. That sweet potato pie ain't gonna eat itself."

Together they walked back to the house, Synthia glowing bright yellow with joy.

The Rescue of Filmore Parish

Mother Diane Simpson took a puff of her Cuban cigar before placing it in her porcelain clamshell ashtray and answering her office door. Sister Carolyn stood on the opposite side, the stout woman's usually jovial face as serious as the situation at hand.

"Still no word?" Mother Diane asked.

"None," Sister Carolyn replied.

Mother Diane sighed. "Assemble the sisters. Meet me in the dining hall in ten minutes."

"Yes, mother."

Mother Diane returned to her desk and finished her cigar. It wasn't unusual to lose contact with a parish. The days were uncertain, and a simple technical breakdown could last for months. But something felt different this time. She couldn't put her finger on it, but something wasn't right. If there was one thing Mother Diane knew, it was never to ignore her instincts. They were always right.

The sisters waited when she entered the sparse dining hall. Mother Diane wasn't one for elaborate accoutrements. She liked things simple, and Celestine Parish Convent was a mirror of her whims. The previous convent director, Mother Patricia Holmes, was the exact opposite. The convent teemed with religious items and other artifacts, something that was impractical in the current times. The sisters had to be prepared to evacuate at a moment's notice, and packing hundreds of frivolous trinkets would mean death for them all.

The sisters stood at attention until Mother Diane reached her seat at the head of the table. She sat then nodded for the others to do the same. All complied except Sister Marie. The tall, lithe woman waited until everyone was seated before speaking.

"Mother Diane, I have grim news from Filmore Parish. It seems the entire parish is under attack."

"Who is it this time?" The Southern Disciples? The Athens Anarchists?" She shifted in her seat, expressing her agitation. "Why do they have names anyway? Like this is a game!"

Sister Marie didn't answer the rhetorical question. Instead, she waited for Mother Diane to settle. That's why Diane liked her. She was sensitive to her moods.

"We have reached out to our usual contacts and have received very little details. Honestly, they seemed very reluctant to share information. It's as if . . ."

Sister Marie stopped speaking.

"As if what?" Mother Diane asked.

"As if they're terrified," Sister Marie replied.

Mother Diane's gut twisted. She placed her palms on the table then pushed herself up, fighting the weariness that threatened to keep her seated.

"Put together a reconnaissance team," she said to Sister Marie.

"Who will be in command?" Sister Marie asked.

"Me," Mother Diane replied.

She marched away from the table. She couldn't send anyone else on this assignment. She had a feeling that whatever they discovered she needed to see with her own eyes.

* * *

Mother Diane strode into the convent courtyard an hour after the dining room meeting. She wore standard issue battle fatigues with ammo belts crisscrossing her chest atop her bulletproof vest. She carried her black helmet adorned with the white cross in the center; her habit still on her head covering her locks. Her AR-15 bounced off her back in time with her wide gait. When she saw the team assembled by the armored Humvee she smiled. Sister Marie had made wise choices. Waiting for her was Sister Joan, Sister Kecia, Sister Rachelle, Sister Elena and Sister Faith. Seeing the young women dressed and armed took her memory back to her days before joining the convent ten long years ago, two years before the Collapse. She was Special Forces Lieutenant Simpson in those days. She was at the top of her game, and she was totally burned out. When retirement came, she jumped at the opportunity, totally ignoring the pleas of her superiors to reconsider. She was spent, so much so that she renewed her faith and became a nun. Because of her real-world skills and devotion, she moved up the ranks rapidly, becoming Mother of the convent when Mother Patricia passed away. Then the Collapse happened, and everything changed.

Mother Diane narrowed her eyes, focusing on Sister Elena.

"Okay Elena, let me see it," she said.

"See what?" Elena replied with false ignorance.

"You know what I'm talking about. Show it to me."

Elena winked. She reached behind her back then revealed her Bowie knife.

"I feel safer already," Mother Diane said.

The other ladies chuckled. Mother Diane gave them a few seconds before her serious expression silenced them.

"This is a reconnaissance mission," she said. "Something's going on in Filmore Parish and we're going to find out. The goal is only to observe. If we encounter hostiles, we will avoid engagement at all costs."

"Since when did we do that?" Sister Joan asked.

Mother Diane frowned. Sister Joan was trigger happy, a shoot-now-ask-questions-later kind of a woman. Sometimes she regretted training her.

"Since today," Diane replied. "Information gathering only."

"So why are you coming?" Sister Kecia asked.

"Because I want to," Mother Diane replied. "Okay ladies, load up. Let's go."

The women climbed into the Black Humvee with Sister Faith at the wheel. They exited the convent then headed for the two-lane highway leading to the county. The people living near the convent waved as they passed, and Mother Diane waved back filled with pride. They were safe because of the sisters; not just because they prayed with them, but because they protected them. She remembered how Mother Patricia frowned on her teaching the sisters self-defense.

"Our lives are in God's hands, not our own," she would say.

"But aren't our hands the extension of His?" Diane would reply.

Mother Patricia thought her response was amusing and allowed her to continue. After the Collapse, the world turned grimmer. Diane stepped up the training to handheld weapons, then eventually to firearms. The government was no more; they could only depend on themselves. A few years before she died, Mother Patricia gave Diane permission to create para-military teams designed to protect the convent from roving bands of thieves, mercenaries and other predators hoping to take advantage of the wives of the Almighty.

The roads became unusable once they crossed into Filmore Parish. The destitute territory was like other nearby parishes; without organized leadership all had fallen into disrepair except those controlled by the sisters and various warlords. They took to the medians and worked their way through the pine-wooded gaps, eventually reaching the Filmore Parish church at dusk. Seeing the abandoned and ruined building brought a shadow over Mother Diane's face. Memories of the day the church was destroyed came back to her and she forced back the tears. Her remembrances were not of the actual attack; thanks be to God she was not there to witness it. Surely, she would have been among the dead. It was the aftermath she saw with the other nuns. The story it told became a nightmare that infected her for years. It was then she defied Mother Patricia's decree and began training the sister in special forces tactics. She purchased weapons and ammunition with Church silver from black market dealers, building a formidable arsenal. But for some sisters what she taught them was not enough. They broke from the convent and went their own way, vowing to bring the wrath of God down on anyone that threated God's flock. They were rarely spoken of.

Sister Faith had barely parked the Humvee when survivors burst from the surrounding woods, crying and wailing in gratitude. They made the sign of the Cross then fell at the sisters' feet.

"Set up camp and distribute supplies," Mother Diane said. She reached down to the bedraggled man at her feet and lifted him to his knees.

"I'm Mother Diane. What..."

The man flung his arms around her neck, almost pulling her to the ground. He sobbed into her uniform for a few moments before drawing away to share a grateful gaze.

"You came! We prayed for you, and you came!"

Mother Diane eased the man down then knelt before him.

"Tell me what happened."

Tears came to the man's eyes again. "They came during the night. Those they could not capture they tried to kill. My house was far away, so I heard the attack when it began. I fled to the woods and hid with the others. We have been hiding for days."

The man took a quick glance around the camp.

"Are more of you coming?" he asked.

"Should there be?" Diane asked in return.

They man nodded vigorously.

"Yes, many more. They are not alone. They have demons with them. The demons . . . the demons ate who they caught."

Mother Diane jumped to her feet.

"Are you sure that's what you saw? It was night, and you were afraid."

The man trembled. "I'm sure. One of them snatched my Maria from my arms and ate her in front of me. There was nothing I could do. Nothing!"

The man collapsed onto his face then cried. Diane was already walking away, fighting to hide her own terror. She saw the same look on the sisters faces who had spoken with the other survivors. Sister Kecia said it before she could.

"There's been a breach."

"Some damn fool didn't think God's protection was enough," Sister Joan replied.

"We're going to need more nuns," Mother Diane said. "And send word to the Daughters of St. Anne."

"The Daughters of St. Anne?" Sister Faith said. "Do you think it's that serious?"

"Demons eating people? That's pretty serious in my book," Mother Diane replied.

Sister Faith climbed inside the Humvee to contact the convent. Mother Diane stuck her head inside.

"When you contact the Daughters, let me talk to Mother Chastity."

"Gladly," Sister Faith replied.

"The rest of you get these people fed. Move them inside the ruins. We can defend ourselves better here than in the woods. At least we'll see them coming. And switch to anointed ammunition."

All the sisters complied with her orders except Sister Joan. She strolled to the edge of the ruins, her eyes sweeping the forest perimeter. Mother Diane went to her side.

"I knew you'd take watch."

Sister Joan smirked while keeping her eyes on the forest.

"They know we're here," she said. "I wouldn't be surprised if they did this just to draw us out."

"Me, either," Mother Diane said.

"So why did we come? We can defend the convent better."

"We had to search for survivors."

Sister Joan stole a glance at Mother Diane.

"I once had a priest tell me our job was to save souls, not lives."

"That was a very callous priest," Mother Diane replied. "Besides, you didn't have to come."

"Of course, I did," Sister Joan replied. "I'm your best fighter, and any chance I have for revenge I take."

"A sister shouldn't harbor such thoughts," Mother Diane admonished.

"But I'm no ordinary sister, am I Mother Diane?"

A chill swept Mother Diane.

"No, you're not. Keep an eye out. Give us a warning when they come. Don't try to take them all yourself."

Sister Joan gave Diane a weak nod. "I will, Mother."

"Mother Diane!" Sister Faith shouted. "I have Mother Chastity."

Diane walked away, glancing at Sister Joan. She didn't lie; she was her best fighter. But Sister Joan came to the convent under odd circumstances. She was well known in the region as a Vodun priestess, and her powers were well respected. The day she arrived begging for refuge she was not the woman all feared. She was starving and bruised. The sisters never asked her how she came to be in such a state and she never offered an explanation. Joan took to her vows and commands seriously, and soon found herself a nun. Mother Patricia displayed her to non-believers as the perfect example of conversion. She was the only one in the convent that didn't know Sister Joan didn't give up her old ways. She had come for protection from whomever or whatever had almost killed her. Diane's training was the other reason.

Diane reached the Humvee. She took a moment to steel herself before taking the radio.

"God be with you, Mother Chastity," she said.

"Our Father is certainly not with you," Mother Chastity replied.

"I don't have time for your insults," Mother Diane said. "We need your help. Someone in Filmore Parish has opened a breach. I need you to close it."

"We will be there," Mother Chasity replied. "But not until first light. It will take us considerable time to prepare."

"We don't have that kind of time. We might not survive the night."

"Then you will meet our Lord and Savior before us all. I am envious of you."

Mother Diane put her hand over her mouth to hold back the curse words.

"You have no choice," Mother Chasity continued. "First light is as soon as we can arrive, if you want us to do what is required properly. I assure you we will be there."

"Thank you, Mother Chasity. We will be anxiously awaiting your arrival."

"God be with you," Mother Chasity said before breaking contact.

Diane handed the radio back to Sister Faith then stomped away. She still wasn't certain that Mother Chasity wasn't delaying her arrival on purpose. There was no love lost between them. Still, there was nothing she could do about it.

The other nuns arrived at dark, their force of six now forty-six. It was still less than Diane desired but it would have to do. The priority was to protect the convent, so the bulk of the nuns remained there. With the help of the surviving locals, they constructed a barrier with the ruins of the church then hunkered down for the inevitable attack. The nuns brought heavy machine guns and rocket launchers; the Humvee was positioned in the center, allowing the 20mm cannon to sweep in any direction. The nuns were spread evenly along the perimeter, their eyes on the woods. Sister Joan stood on the makeshift ramparts fully exposed. There was nothing left for them to do but wait. Mother Diane returned to the Humvee, worn out by the stress. She lay prone in the carriage and closed her eyes. She needed the rest. It was going to be a long night.

It was the silence that woke her. Mother Diane sat up, put on her night vision goggles, grabbed her AR-15 and ran to the ramparts.

"Sound the alarm!" she shouted. "They're here!"

Gunfire erupted from the forest edge and the nuns quickly answered, gun barrels flashing while tracer rounds from the 20mm streaked into the darkness. Mother Diane ran to the ramparts where Sister Joan guarded but did not see her. She reached the broken stone barricade and heard grunting and cursing. Without hesitation she jumped the ramparts to see the sister fighting off three of the flesh eaters, wielding her silver infused machetes with precise efficiency. Ashes flew where her blade struck home, blurring the space between them. But Diane could see enough. She blasted one of the demons through the skull and it exploded into cinders. A second silver bullet shattered the leg of another demon; Sister Joan decapitated it before it could hit the ground. The third broke way, bounding for the tree line. A 20mm round smacked into its back, blowing it into powder.

"Come on!" Diane shouted as she grabbed Sister Joan's arm and dragged her over the ramparts. Bullets ricocheted off the stones and buzzed past their heads as they hunkered down and joined the firefight. Sister Elena crawled to them, blood running from her arm.

"It's nothing," she said before Mother Diane asked. "Mother, we should get the anointed ammo to our best markswomen. Every shot must count."

"Do it," Diane said. She fired a few rounds into the face of a man close to the battlements. "Get some of the civilians to help. It's their asses we're saving."

Sister Elena ignored her verbal slip. She left four clips of anointed ammo with Diane and Joan then crawled away.

The firefight kept up throughout the night, their attackers relentless. There was no time for rest or relief. Twice the ramparts were almost breached, but concentrated fire from the 20mm and the heavy machine guns saved them. Yet every hour a nun was lost. They were down to half their number as the sun rose over the loblolly pines and live oaks.

Mother Diane and the others continue the fight, holding back exhaustion with prayers and grit. Diane was drawing a bead on a demon when she noticed it. The higher the sun rose, the more erratic it became. The other demons acted the same. They stumbled toward the tree line away from the rising sun.

"That's why she waited," Mother Diane whispered.

Her sentence was punctuated by the woosh of rockets. Two huge explosions ripped the ground before them, men and demons flung into the air. Diane heard the familiar thumping and turned her head to the east, shading her eyes with her hand. Two white Huey Cobras flanked a troop transport VTOL, the three airships approaching like raptors after prey. The gatling guns on the Cobras spewed blessed rounds into the attackers, clearing a space for the transport VTOL to land. Its wheels touch ground the hatches dropped open, unleashing the Daughters of St. Anne. As much as Mother Diane didn't want to admit, they made an impressive sight in their white fatigues, and silver crosses gleaming in the center of their black helmets. The first Daughters out of the VTOL brandished M6o machine guns, sweeping the area to make way for the other sisters. They quickly formed an advance formation and began driving the attackers into the woods. Diane smiled. She'd taught them well.

The nuns cheered as they watch their cohorts break the horde. None joined the fight; they were exhausted and deserved a reprieve. Diane was about to check on them when a small observation copter landed nearby the VTOL. The door swung open, and Mother Chastity emerged, dressed in a traditional nun habit, her only symbol of rank the golden cross hanging from her neck. The two women approached each other, sharing a perfunctory hug.

"I told you we would come," Mother Chastity said.

"When it was most convenient to you," Diane replied.

"You taught me well."

Diane nodded at the VTOLs.

"How did you get the air support?"

Mother Chastity shared her pencil thin grin. "They were a gift."

"What warlord did you kill?"

"It was a donation," Chasity replied. "In return we spared his stronghold. God is good."

"All the time," Mother Diane replied.

Mother Chastity grinned then looked over her shoulder.

"How many have received the glory of our Savior's presence?"

"Twenty," Diane replied.

Chastity nodded. "A small price to pay for holy ground."

Diane kept quiet. This was not the time to argue.

"Our task is not complete," Chastity said. "The demons flee to their hovel. We will drive them inside then seal the breach with Holy silver. Would you like to witness?"

"I would," Sister Joan said. The sister limped to them, machetes in hand.

"Ah, of course you would. But you won't need those. We're not getting that close."

Mother Chastity marched to the observation copter. She reached inside then extracted a Dragunov sniper rifle. Diane shook her head.

"Another donation?"

Chastity ignored her comment.

"I have two, Sister Joan. Would you like to join me?"

Sister Joan's eyes sparkled.

"Of course!"

The women climbed into the copter. Diane trotted away as the rotors gained speed. She had lost another nun to the Sisters; of that, she was sure. But she would not dwell on it. There was dead to bury and wounded to tend. Things would eventually get back to normal, at least for a time. Until then, she would be about God's work, by any means necessary.

-End-

The Warriors of Mogai

The bush deer stood motionless, its ears twitching as it listened with the clarity of sight. Patience was its defense against the predators of the bush, a stillness that rivaled that of the towering ironwoods under which it hid. The hunter would eventually falter, and the deer would dart into the underbrush to safety. But Koboye was no mere hunter. He crouched, as still as a stone, his arms locked in place, his fingers pinching the bowstring and arrow as he held his breath.

The bush deer sniffed, then dropped its head to nibble the leaves of a nearby shrub. Koboye released the bowstring, and the arrow flew true, striking the deer just behind its front leg. The deer fell to its side and died almost instantly, the arrow piercing its **heart and lungs.**

Koboye waited a few breaths before hurrying to his kill. He twisted the arrow then pulled it free before lifting the deer from the ground, throwing it over his narrow shoulders then running away as fast as he could from the spot where the beast fell. He knew scavengers would soon smell the scent of a fresh kill and converge. He hoped to be far away before that occurred.

It took him ten minutes to reach the hunting camp. The others were processing the beasts he'd slain earlier that day. Their singing, laughing, and arguing as he approached brought a smile to his weary face. Inira, his eldest sister, looked up from her boiling pot and greeted him with a smile.

"Koboye! Are you trying to kill all the bush deer?"

Koboye smiled back. "Only those that sleep when they see me."

They shared a laugh with the others. Koboye placed the deer on the ground and the women converged on the carcass with their knives. Mumbi approached him, avoiding his eyes before speaking.

"Did you use a poisoned arrow?" she asked.

"No," he replied. "This was a clean kill."

Mumbi looked up and smiled. Their eyes met and Koboye felt his heart stir.

"That is good," she said. "It will take less time to process."

"Get away from my brother!"

Inira ran at Mumbi, chasing her away with a stirring stick.

"Why did you do that?" he asked.

"Mama and baba have already chosen a wife for you," Inira said.

Curiosity rounded Koboye's eyes. "Who?"

"You will know when the time comes," Inira said.

"Why would they tell you?"

"They didn't," Inira replied. "I'm a good listener."

Inira pointed at the bush.

"Go back and bring more bush meat," she said. "A warthog would be good. Maybe two."

Koboye sighed and trudged back into the bush. Inira was his oldest sister, but she treated him like he was her child. He respected her because she was his elder, but sometimes he wanted to yell at her. But she would tell mama and baba, and that wouldn't end well.

The hunting spirits were with him. Not only did he kill a warthog, but he also bagged another bush deer. The camp took time to thank the spirits for the bounty, then celebrated with dancing and singing before the evening meal. After eating, Koboye went off alone to perform his secret libations to the spirits that guided his bow and spear.

"What are you doing?"

Koboye whirled about to see Mumbi standing with her hands behind her back and an innocent smile on her face.

"I can't say," he said. "And you cannot see."

"Ah, you are pouring libations," she said.

Koboye's eyes widened.

"How do you know?"

"My baba is a hunter too, remember? But he is not as good as you."

She walked up and sat beside him.

"Baba says the ancestors favor you. He says the animal spirits respect you, too. That is why they give themselves to you so freely."

Koboye turned away so Mumbi would not see his smile.

"I don't know the will of the spirits," he said. "I can only thank them for their benevolence."

"You are humble too," Mumbi said. "That is why I want to marry you. You will be a good husband and will be a good wife."

"You know that's not our decision," Koboye said.

"I told my baba I want to marry you," she replied. "I told him to make sure my bride-price is not too high."

"You said that? What did he say?"

Mumbi smiled. "My baba loves me above all else. He is meeting with your baba while we are away. I'm sure they will come to an agreement, for your baba loves you and knows I'll make a good wife."

Mumbi reached and touched his cheek.

"We will be happy and have many children."

She stood, shared another smile, then walked away. Koboye watched her for a moment before returning to his ritual. But he couldn't do it. He couldn't concentrate. Mumbi's visit took his mind to another place. How could she be so certain of the future? She had just reached the age of womanhood as he had of manhood, yet she was sure of a future Koboye could not see beyond the next hunt. It was as if the ancestors were blinding him to his destiny.

The next day they broke down the hunting camp and began their journey home. The bush diminished as the grasses exerted their dominance. After two days the mud walls of Kisamu rose over the horizon. As much as Koboye enjoyed the solitude of the bush, he was happy to be home. Hunting was a harsh life; to wake up to a warm bowl of sorghum and his mama's attention was a salve to his body and spirit.

The farmers were the first to spot their group and rushed to meet them, ready to barter for the fresh bush meat.

"Go away!" Inira shouted as she brandished her club. "You must wait until we reach the market!"

A tall, stout woman approached Inira, ignoring his sister's threatening gestures.

"Why should we wait, child?" she asked. "We have items to barter and cowries to pay now."

Inira's attitude receded before the woman.

"Aunt Bompaka, if I were to sell or trade any of this meat with you, my parents would punish me. They would think me a bad daughter."

Bompoka tapped her foot while scrutinizing their group.

"Go on then," she finally said. "But we will follow you so we can get first choice."

They proceeded to the city, their followers growing. The closer they came, the more nervous Koboye became. By the time they entered the city, he was wringing his hands.

"I don't think he's here."

Inira's voice startled him.

"I wasn't looking for him," he said.

"Stop lying, you're always looking for him so you can avoid him," she said. "One day you're just going to have to punch Kone in the mouth. Just like I did."

"Kone won't hit you back," Koboye said. "Baba would beat him."

Inira shrugged. "Relax, Koboye. Our annoying brother isn't here. He and the other boys take the cattle to the high pastures during this season, remember? He won't be back for at least a moon."

Koboye sighed. He continued walking to the market with the others, happy he wouldn't have to deal with Kone and his friends. The older boys loved to tease his age group and followed Kone's every word. It was easy to see why. Kone was tall, broad shouldered and handsome. And he was the best wrestler in the city, even better than men much older than him. The ancestors blessed Koboye with a hunter's spirit; they gave Kone the soul of a fighter.

They finally reached the market. There was a surge of people around them, each shouting out what they would pay or trade for fresh bush meat. Inira regained her haughty attitude, shouting down the over eager and swinging her club at anyone attempting to take a portion from their baskets. It was a relief when they reached mama's booth. His aunts waded into the throng, forcing everyone into a line that stretched to the edge of the market. Mama came from behind the stall, wrapped in a colorful kanga that exposed her left shoulder. She smiled at

Koboye then hurried to him, taking his cheeks in her hands then kissing his nose.

"The great hunter has returned," she said. "You did well, I see."

"The ancestors were generous," Koboye replied.

"You always say that," mama said. "The ancestors did not pull back the bowstring and let the arrow fly."

"But they guided the arrow true and convinced the bush deer to give up its soul," Koboye replied.

Mama shook her head. "You can't be a hunter and a medicine priest, too."

Mama tickled him and he laughed.

"I will help you," he said.

Mama shook her head. "Inira and I can handle this. Your baba needs to see you. You must go to him immediately."

"Is he home?"

"No. He's at the elders' lodge."

"The elders' lodge?"

Mama turned him around then gave him a slight push.

"Hurry. They've been waiting for you for a long time."

Koboye shrugged. What would the elders want with him? He made his way through the market crush, finding the path leading to the lodge at the head of the village. The oblong structure rested under the branches of the ancestor tree, the tallest and widest plant on the grasslands for strides. He stopped at the base of the tree, opened his gourd, and poured libations in respect before knocking on the lodge door.

"Who is it?"

"Koboye."

The door opened revealing his baba's somber face.

"My son," he said. "Come inside."

Koboye lowered his head and entered the elders' lodge. A small fire burned in the center, its smoke rising like a translucent column through a circular opening in the roof. The elders sat in a semi-circle, their weathered faces emotionless. Koboye had never been so close to them. He hoped they didn't see his shaking hands. Baba sat at the right end of the elders.

"Sit Koboye," Kuhungu, the elder on the left said.

Koboye prostrated before them before crossing his legs and sitting.

"Koboye, do you know why you are here?" Kuhungu asked.

"No, uncle," I do not," Koboye answered.

"What do you know of the warriors of Mogai?"

Koboye looked at his baba.

"Nothing."

Kuhungu frowned. "You lie."

"It's okay, Koboye," his baba said. "You can tell them."

Koboye's throat went dry. He swallowed before speaking.

"Baba used to tell us a story of the warriors of Mogai. He said that long ago, our people lived in the mountains alongside them, but we would war all the time. Weary of fighting, our chiefs came to an agreement. Our people would leave the mountains and live in the grasslands. And the warriors of Mogai promised to aid us from the threats of the desert people."

"This is no story," Kuhungu said. "It is our history, passed down from jele to jele. The desert folk do not come with frequency. As a matter of fact, the last time we saw them, and the warriors, was the dry season of our grandfathers' grandfathers. But the signs are here. The rains have been few, and the desert oases are surely drying. They will come soon."

"As will the warriors?" Koboye asked.

Kuhungu looked away. "We do not know."

"So, who will protect us from the desert folk?"

"This is why you are here," Kuhungu said. "There was a time when the desert folk were near, but the warriors were absent. A messenger was sent to find them and lead them to us. The messenger was a hunter, like you."

Koboye's eyes went to his baba. Baba looked back with concern. This was a great responsibility, one too great for a man like him who only weeks ago was a boy. But he knew the elders would not change their minds.

"When must I leave?" he asked.

"Immediately," Kuhungu said.

Koboye nodded. "Does the jele know the song that will show me the way?"

The elders stirred and Baba spoke.

"No."

Koboye's mouth dried so much that it pained him to speak.

"Then how will I find them?"

Kuhungu reached behind his back, revealing an ebonywood box.

"With this."

Koboye stood then approached the elder to receive the box.

"Open it," the elder said.

Koboye lifted the lid. Inside was a small figurine carved from ivory in the shape of a warrior riding a beast which resembled a large donkey.

"It is Tumaini," Kuhungu said. "It will guide you to the warriors."

Koboye took Tumaini in his hand. He felt its energy, the constant vibration stirring his waning confidence. He closed the box and put it in his bag.

"There is a donkey loaded with provisions waiting for you at your home," Kuhungu said. "Your baba will take you. Say your goodbyes to your family and be on your way."

Koboye prostrated to the elders again then crawled backwards until he reached the entrance. He stood and exited the lodge house. Baba emerged moments later.

"Come," he said. "We don't have much time."

"Baba, I'm not ready for this," he said.

"No one is ready," baba replied. "But if you do not find the warriors, we will all die."

Koboye shivered with baba's last words. He wanted to run away and hide in the bush until the elders were forced to pick someone else, someone older and wiser. But baba's stare convinced him that he must at least try.

Koboye followed baba to their family compound. Most of his relatives were at the market, but his older aunts, uncles and cousins were doing simple chores and watching the children. They greeted Koboye with ululations and waves, and Koboye tried his best to seem happy. But his mind was in turmoil.

Baba took him to their house. The donkey was tethered to a small bush, loaded with bags of provisions. Koboye inspected each bag and his nervousness increased.

"This is enough for many moons," Koboye said. "Do you expect it to take this long?"

"We don't know," baba said. "I know you can fend for yourself, but I don't want you to use too much energy hunting. Save it for your journey."

Koboye inspected his provisions one more time then untethered the donkey.

"One more thing," baba said. "Follow me."

Koboye and baba entered the house. Baba went to the bed he shared with mama then knelt. He reached under the mat then pulled out a blanket bundle. He handed the bundle to Koboye.

"This is for you," he said.

Koboye opened the bundle. Inside was a long piece of iron, with a sharpened curve at the top. The iron was well oiled; baba had taken meticulous care of it. Koboye wasn't sure, but this resembled some sort of weapon.

"What is it?" he asked.

"It is a muder," baba said. "Long ago, when our people were warriors, this was the weapon we used. You can strike with it as well as throw it, like the throwing clubs you use to hunt. Except this is for men."

"Why are you giving this to me?"

"You may need it," baba said. "No one knows what lies between us and Mogai. I was going to give this to Kone one day, but it is you that deserves it."

Koboye wrapped the muder then took it outside, securing it to the donkey. He was glad Kone was not here to see baba give it to him. There was already enough animosity between them. This would probably be too much for his self-centered brother to bear.

When Koboye turned around, baba stood before him. They hugged, longer and tighter than they ever had.

"Farewell son," he said. "Find the warriors and bring them back. Our lives depend on it."

Baba's last words sent a shiver down his legs. He put his hand on the donkey to steady himself.

"Baba, I don't know . . ."

"Pray when you need to," baba said. "The ancestors and spirits are with you. We are too."

"Say goodbye to mama, Inira, and Kone for me."

Koboye hugged baba one more time then went on his way, leading the donkey towards the bush. He looked ahead; Mogai's snow covered peak barely broke the eastern horizon. From the village it was barely visible, but Koboye was blessed with hunter's eyes. It would be a long journey, but he would make it. He had to.

* * *

Darkness weighed heavy on the humid night, obscuring the boundary between the sky and the thick forest canopy. The light from Koboye's fire barely illuminated his dour umber face as he poked at the embers with his muder hoping to stir up the flames. The charred wood refused to give up its essence easily. His donkey, unburdened from its load, wandered in the nearby bush as it foraged for food. Koboye had hunted alone in these woods many times but this night the isolation agitated him. Kisamu was not far behind him, but it felt like it was a thousand strides away. No matter how distant he travelled he always knew he would return home. This time he was not so sure.

The night sounds of the bush played a rhythm he knew well. He tried to relax, laying his head on a thick branch, his weapons by his side. The fire would keep the curious night beasts away. He hoped his prayers and the ancestors would protect him from those bolder. His eyes drifted to the box resting near his pack. Inside was Tumaini. Maybe it would protect him, too. According to the elders it was powerful gris gris. He hoped so.

Despite Koboye's uneasiness sleep finally found him, but only briefly. Something moved in the bush. He jumped into a crouch, grabbed his bow, and notched an arrow as his eyes darted from left to right. After a moment he knew what caused the commotion was human. No beast would travel though the bush making such noise unless it was being chased.

"Koboye?" The familiar voice shocked him. At first, he thought the spirits played games with him. He kept his bow raised and remained silent.

"Koboye?"

The voice was loud, insistent, and arrogant. He then knew it wasn't the spirits. He frowned as he lowered his bow.

"Kone, here," Koboye called.

Kone crashed through the bush and into the firelight. Koboye's brother carried an assegai in his right hand with a provision bag slung over his shoulder. His short sword, his *bakatwa*, hung from his waist in its wooden sheath while he chopped at a stray vine with his *gano*. He grinned as he approached and Koboye's nervousness grew. It was never good when Kone smiled.

The brothers stood face to face. Kone was only three years older than Koboye but towered over his younger brother. Some said Kone was a warrior spirit reborn from a time when the baKisamu were conquerors, not farmers. In those days they did not need the protection of the warriors of Mogai. He was the strongest boy of his age group and constantly proved it in wrestling matches that he easily won.

"I knew I would find you," Kone said. "See, I'm not as bad a tracker as you think."

"I did not say that," Koboye answered.

"You didn't have to." Kone pushed by Koboye, dropped his weapons and bag then sat before the fire. Koboye gazed at his brother's back, thinking about the question he wished to ask out loud.

Why are you here, Kone?

"Baba misses you," Kone said as he warmed his hands over the fire. "He'll be glad to know you're okay."

"I'm not far from Kisamu. I know these woods."

They were silent for a moment until Koboye's curiosity overwhelmed his apprehension.

"Kone, why are you here?"

Kone peered over his shoulder. "I was worried about you. I came to escort you to the edge of the forest. When I feel you are safe, I'll go back home."

"I'm fine," Koboye said.

"I know you are," Kone replied. "But I'm your elder brother. I'm responsible for you."

Koboye would have laughed out loud if he had not been afraid of how Kone would respond.

"It's late," Koboye finally said. "If we wish to make the forest edge by nightfall tomorrow, we need to rest. It will be a hard walk."

"Do you have anything to eat?" Kone asked.

"What did you bring?" Koboye replied.

Kone reached into his bag and took out two old yams. It was a clear sign his brother had come in haste. Knowing Kone, he refused to eat them despite the fact he was famished. Koboye went to his bag and handed his brother the fresh wild yams he'd dug up a day earlier. Kone's eyes widened as he smiled.

"Thank you!" He dusted the yams quickly then devoured them. Koboye laid back down in frustration. He would have to forage again once he reached the forest edge.

"Do have anything else?" Kone asked.

"No," Koboye snapped. "It is late, Kone. We'll gather more in the morning. That should be enough for tonight."

"How do you know what's enough for me?" Kone's voice was stern, just the way Koboye was used to. He felt comfort in his brother's anger. At least he was now sure that it was his brother and not a mischievous wood spirit.

"It will have to do. It's all I had."

"Oh. Well, good night brother."

Koboye tucked the muder close. "Good night, Kone."

The chattering of agitated primates and curious birds stirred Koboye from his slumber. He awoke to his brother standing over him, his bulk blocking the morning sunlight. He held Tumaini in his right hand. Kone stared at the object with a smug look on his face as he absently nodded his head.

"What are you doing?" Koboye asked.

Kone jerked. "Oh, nothing. Just admiring our savior. Such a small object to bear such a large burden."

Koboye snatched the idol from Kone and placed it back into its box. He glared at his brother.

"Baba told you," Koboye said.

"Everyone told me," Kone replied. "It was all anyone could talk about after we returned from the pastures."

"It is not a toy," Koboye said as he put the box back into his bag.

"Why are you worried?" Kone asked. "No one would dare approach the two of us. We are warriors."

Koboye ignored the sarcasm in his brother's comment. It was past time for Kone to go home. Koboye said nothing as he gathered his things. The two walked in silence through the thick brush. They stopped at midday; Koboye went hunting, returning with two monkeys and more wild yams. After a tense meal they continued. The bush thinned toward sunset, a sign they were nearing the end of the forest. By the time the savannah came into view the sun sat low on the horizon, its light muted.

"Thank you for your escort," Koboye said to Kone. "You should head back now while you can still find the way."

"I'm not going back," Kone said. "You are."

Kone's words hit Koboye like a blow in the back. He turned to face his brother. Kone stood in his familiar fighting stance, his hands on his hips, his head slightly tilted back.

"The elders were wrong. You are not the one to deliver Tumaini to the Mogai. Yes, you are a good hunter and all that, but what will these noble warriors think when they see you? I'll tell you what they'll think. They'll think we are a weak people that don't deserve their time, let alone their protection."

"You'll defy the elders?" Koboye fought back the fury building in his head. Kone was bigger and stronger than him.

Kone laughed. "No matter how upset they may be when you return their anger will disappear when I return with the Mogai. They are warriors. They expect a warrior to come for them."

Kone extended his hand. "Give me Tumaini and go home, Koboye."

Koboye took his bag off his shoulder then threw it behind him.

"No."

Kone's eyes narrowed. "Don't be foolish, you can't expect . . ."

Koboye took the muder off his shoulder. "I said no."

Kone smiled. He dropped his bag and took out his sword and axe. "You don't want to play this game, brother."

Koboye charged Kone, the anger of years of abuse unleashed. Kone blocked Koboye's wild swing and dodged to the right. Koboye's barely avoided Kone's foot sweep as he jumped and stumbled. He spun to see Kone's smug face.

"Give me Tumaini, Koboye."

Koboye gripped the muder and circled Kone. His hands felt warm on the weapon's grip, a sensation that worked its way up his wrists and into his arms. A rhythm pulsed in his veins, and he smiled. It was the beat of the stick dance, the ritual he and his baba always performed for the bearers after a successful hunt. Baba told him before he left on his journey that the stick dance was also the dance of the muder. But it was more. The ancestors spoke to him through the iron, the hammers of the sacred smiths beating in time with his heart. There was no doubt that this was his task.

When Koboye attacked his brother again his moves were fluid and controlled. With every blow the muder became lighter in his hands. Kone's frustration was clear in his face as Koboye spun, dodged, struck, and retreated. He did not hit Kone, only his weapons, and Kone could not strike him.

Kone's frustration spilled into action. He launched a furious attack, sword, and axe blurring. Koboye was lost in the dance, blocking Kone's weapons with ease. The fight was nearing its climax. It was time for it to end. Koboye spun, knocking Kone's sword and axe from each hand. He spun once more, the muder's edge heading for Kone's neck. Koboye twisted the weapon and pulled it down. It smacked Kone's forearm. There was a loud crack and Kone cried out. He fell to his knees.

Koboye stopped, his chest heaving. Kone held his broken forearm, staring at Koboye in shock and fear. Koboye secured the muder over his shoulder and went to his wounded brother.

"Stay away from me! You broke my arm!"

Koboye said nothing as he knelt by his brother. "Let me see."

Kone extended his injured arm and Koboye touched it gently.

"It's not as bad as it could have been," he said. He picked up Kone's axe and went to a stand of nearby trees. He returned with two thick branches. With a section of rope from his bag he made a sturdy splint.

"This should keep your arm stable. When you get back, find Nzila. She is very good at healing broken bones."

"I can't go back alone!" Kone cried. "My arm is broken!"

"You came here alone for your own reasons," Koboye said. "The Elders and the ancestors chose me to deliver Tumaini to the Mogai. Whether you make it back is not my concern. Goodbye, Kone."

Koboye gathered his provisions and set out for the river. There was a twinge of guilt in his chest, but it did not linger. He was on a quest to save

Kisamu. The life of a self-centered brother was small in comparison.

"I hope you fail!" Kone shouted.

Koboye stopped. He turned to look at his brother.

"For your own sake and the sake of our people, you should hope otherwise."

*   *   *

Koboye and the donkey continued their journey to Mogai. As the mountain rose higher before them, the clouds overhead became thicker and heavier. Rainy season was coming. Koboye wished it had been the same for Kisamu and the desert, for he would not be on this desperate journey to save his people. He picked up his pace. They would have to reach the river and cross it soon before the rains came. Otherwise, the current might be too strong and the river too high for them to cross.

He set up camp at dusk on a low rise which gave him a good view of the surrounding savannah. He let the donkey go, and it trotted down the slope to graze on the nearby grasses. As he cleared an area for his sleeping mat, he looked about at the local trees. With rain soon to be upon him, he would need a bark coat. He located a stand of trees and hurried to them, hoping to harvest the bark before nightfall. Reaching the trees, he searched until he found a few mutubas. Its bark was easy to peel and water resistant enough to keep him dry. Koboye took out his gano and cut a vertical crease down the tree. He was about to cut again when he heard a moan. He crouched, his eyes searching the bush for any predator. He heard the groan again. This time it was louder and there was no doubt it was a person.

Koboye used all his stealth as he followed the sound, wary of an ambush. The bush gave way to a small clearing. On the edge of the cover lay a girl. Tears flowed from her eyes; her hands pressed over a jagged wound on her right thigh. The girl whimpered when she saw him and attempted to drag herself away as Koboye approached. He stopped and raised his hands.

"I mean you no harm," he said. "Do you understand me?"

The girl nodded slowly.

Koboye eased closer. He recognized the wound; a simba caused it. It was rare for a simba to attack a person. It must have been old or starving. Koboye took his bag of healing herbs from his hip. It was a bad injury and would take most of what he had, but he could not leave the girl to die. He opened a pouch and sprinkled the sealing dust into his hand.

"This will sting a little, but the pain will go away quickly," he told the girl. He sprinkled the dust on her leg, and she winced.

"I am Koboye," he said. "What is your name?"

The girl looked at him. There was something different about her eyes, a strangeness that unnerved him.

"I am Nguboko," she said.

"Nguboko, where is your family?"

"The simbas chased them away," she replied. "They tried to save me, but there were too many. I was preparing to meet my ancestors when a donkey came along and distracted them."

Koboye's back straightened. "A donkey! Oh no!"

He jumped to his feet, then slowly sat back down. If what Nguboko said was true, the simbas abandoned her for more familiar prey. Although a donkey wasn't an easy kill, it was no match for a pride.

"Was it your donkey?" Nguboko asked.

"I think so."

"I am sorry."

Koboye shrugged. "It's not your fault, only the ancestors' will."

He looked at the lacerations. To his surprise, they were healing.

"Do you think you can walk?"

Nguboko sat up. "I think so."

Koboye helped her stand. She was taller than appeared, her head almost even with his. She put her arm around his shoulder, and he felt her weight. Together they shuffled to his camp where he eased her to the ground.

"Koboye, I'm hungry," she said. "Do you have something to eat?"

"Yes," Koboye said.

He went to his pack, taking out a yam. He was handing it to her when she snatched it from his hand and bit into it.

"You are very hungry," he commented.

Nguboko laughed through a full mouth. "I am."

She finished the yam in minutes.

"Can I have another one?"

Koboye nodded. With the donkey gone, he couldn't carry all the provisions. He would have to leave some behind, so it might as well go to good use. This time Nguboko ate slowly, her eyes fixed on Koboye as he joined her.

"Where are you from, Koboye?" she asked.

"The west. My home is Kisamu."

Nguboko nibbled on her yam. "I have heard of it. It is a great city."

Koboye laughed. "Now you tease me. Kisamu is many things, but great is not one of them."

"It must be, for it is your home."

Koboye was about to laugh again until he saw the seriousness in Nguboko's eyes.

"Who are you really?" he asked.

Nguboko smiled. "I am just a girl that you saved."

She put down her yam and laid on the grass.

"I'm tired."

"Here."

Koboye gave her his sleeping mat.

"Thank you, *bakala*," she said.

"What did you say?" Koboye asked.

"Nothing," Nguboko replied. "You are kind, brave and generous. The baKisamu are richer to have you. I will never forget your kindness."

Nguboko lay down and fell immediately to sleep. Koboye watched her for a moment before laying down as well. He had lost his donkey, but gained a friend, it seemed. His questions could wait until the morning.

Koboye slept well despite the trying day. He awoke to a gray sky that reminded him he had to finish his bark coat before the rain began. He turned on his side to check on Nguboko. She was gone.

"Nguboko!"

Koboye found her tracks easily. He followed them down the hill to the grass. Halfway between the hill and the bush he discovered signs of a struggle. Nguboko's footprints disappeared, replaced by something larger and heavier.

"No!"

Koboye ran across the grass, following the footprints to the bush. Shrubs and small trees had been pushed aside as whatever he followed crashed into the interior. Koboye followed the trail a few moments longer then stopped. Although he saw no blood, he knew there was no way he could save Nguboko. Whatever had taken her had too much of a head start, and even if he did catch up with it, could he confront it? The signs indicated something enormous. He turned then trudged back to the edge of the bush. Locating the tree he had been working on earlier for its bark, he finished removing the layer and returned to his camp. As he pounded the bark with a stone he found nearby, he tried to keep his mind from falling into dark places. Nguboko was gone, as was his donkey. He still had at least a moon before he reached Mogai, and who knew what would happen once he was there. He glanced to the west where his people waited for him to return with the warriors that would protect them from the desert folk. Koboye dropped the stone. He dug his bag and took out Tamani's box. He placed the figure in his palm and was reassured by its warmth. He would put his faith in the ancestors and the spirits. It was all he could do.

The rain began as light sprinkles, annoying and persistent. By midday it was steady and heavier. Koboye donned his raincoat and was pleased. It didn't keep him completely dry, but it was enough to keep him from getting sick. He walked until dusk and was lucky enough to find a tree to climb for the night, a stiff branch better than a soaked ground.

After three days of rain Koboye was careful to avoid patches of thick mud. He kept a steady slow pace, his eyes locked on his feet. There was no reason to look ahead. Mogai seemed to taunt him, daring him to continue. The days passed and the rain grew heavier, forcing Koboye to detour from his path to avoid large waterholes. But then he heard a sound that weighed more despair on his shoulders.

A river raged before him; a swollen brown serpent jumbled with runoff debris. Koboye searched up and down the bank, hoping to find some shallow ford that would make crossing less dangerous but found none. All he saw was huge mambas resting on the bank, waiting to make a meal of any creature foolish or desperate enough to cross.

He had to cross. The rains would fall for moons, and he did not have time to wait for the waters to recede. He secured his provisions as tight as he could to his torso, praying that the extra mass would help his buoyancy. He paced up and down the bank until he found the narrowest point between the banks. Koboye waded into the shallows, the water pressing against his calves.

"Ancestors protect me."

Koboye swam. He did not fight the current; instead, he swam just fast enough to make slow progress. He would reach the other side, but it would take time. The current was swifter than he judged, but he would make it if he did not panic. As he reached the middle of the river, a large branch broke the surface, twisting toward him. Koboye tried to avoid it, but it struck him hard, throwing him into a tumble. He struggled to right himself, flailing against the current as he tried to keep his head above water. As he searched for the bank, he saw what he dreaded. The mambas had seen his struggle and were sliding into the water. Koboye was too far from the opposite bank to return, and the mambas would get him before he reached the opposite bank. Koboye took out his knife. He would not win, but he would fight. That was all he could do.

The mambas converged. Koboye treaded water, his eyes darting from creature to creature. The closest mamba flicked its tail, shooting toward Koboye like an arrow released from a celestial bow. Koboye braced himself. Something struck him from below with a force so hard he rose into the air, splashing down closer to the bank. Before he could swim the water roiled beside him and the huge head of a beast Koboye had never seen emerged from the brown water. It opened its huge mouth, exposing two large tusks on its lower jaw. Koboye waved his knife; the beast surged at him, dropping its head at the last minute and scooping him into its maw. Koboye rolled against its teeth, the tusks trapping him. The upper half of its mouth came down but instead of biting him in two, the beast pressed down just enough to immobilize him. Koboye didn't resist; he did not want to urge the beast to shake him into stillness like he had seen other predators do. The beast plunged under water, taking Koboye with it. Instead of swimming it ran along the river bottom, rising to the surface when Koboye was about to lose breath then diving down to run again. The beast continued until they reached the opposite bank. Koboye's mind raced. Would it devour him now, or was he being carried to a nest or den to be fed to young ones? He hoped for the latter, for at least then he would have a chance to fight himself free.

The beast clambered onto the muddy bank then flicked its head, throwing Koboye free. He landed hard on his side. He rolled onto his knees, his knife pointed at the creature. It was larger than he imagined, larger than a water buffalo, almost as large as a tembo. It stared at him, its nostrils flaring, a low grunt emitting from its huge mouth. Something familiar stirred in its eyes, something that resembled recognition. Koboye was drawn in deeper; the image of a young girl appeared in his mind.

"Nguboko? It cannot be!"

The beast let out a loud grunt, turned away and rumbled into the river. Koboye stood transfixed, attempting to comprehend what just happened. As the beast entered the water, he saw scars on its rear right leg, scars like Nguboko's. The beast returned, this time with his provisions in its mouth. It dropped them at his feet, then pressed its head against him before turning and running to the raging river. It splashed into the currents, Koboye watching until it disappeared under the water.

Koboye knelt and picked up his bag, his eyes riveted on the river as he secured it to his body. He faced Mogai, a smile on his face. At least he knew Nguboko was alive.

* * *

Koboye crouched in tall grass as he watched the people of the village before him go about their daily chores. He spotted the smoke from their fires strides ago and changed his direction because he was starving. The water from the river had ruined his provisions, and his hunting had not gone well. He was not familiar with this land and was not confident in what plants he could or could not eat.

Koboye decided to wait until nightfall, slip into the village and steal enough food to get him to Mogai. Once he reached the warriors, he would depend on their good faith. He could approach the villagers and ask for their hospitality. In the west it would be freely given, but he knew nothing of the people of the east, except for the baMogai, and what he knew of them was from songs of long ago.

Koboye found a dense stand of shrubs, laid out his sleeping mat, and rested until nightfall.

Something rough and wet dragged across Koboye's face, startling him. He opened his eyes to the face of a bovine with large, curved horns looming over him. The beast crooned.

"Ta-ta, what is it?" someone said.

The face of a boy appeared. His eyes widened, then he ran away.

"Stranger! Stranger!"

Koboye clambered to his feet and tried to catch the boy.

"Wait!"

The bovine snorted. Others joined it, forming a circle around Koboye. The boy returned with more boys, each holding a staff. They held their sticks high, threatening expressions on their young, scarred faces. Koboye held up his hands.

"I mean no harm," he said.

The first boy stepped into the horned circle.

"Who are you?" the boy demanded. "Where are you from?"

"I'm Koboye from Kasumi. I have been travelling for many moons. I have no more supplies, and I am very hungry."

"You came to steal from us!" the boy said.

"Yes . . . I mean, no," Koboye replied.

"Why were you hiding in the grass?" the boy asked.

"I . . . I was not hiding."

"Luemba, what are you doing?"

The deep resonant voice came from outside of the circle. The boys scattered away, their herd following them. Twelve stern warriors replaced them. They were bare-chested, wielding spears with broad-leaf heads. Swords hung from their shoulders in wooden scabbards. White tattoos covered their left shoulders. One of the men, the tallest of the group with a thin gray beard stepped up to Koboye.

"I am Mayele," he said.

"I am Koboye."

Mayele tilted his head.

"Koboye, why are you here?"

"I have come from the west," he said. "I seek the warriors of Mogai."

Mayele jumped when Koboye mentioned the mountain's name. He lowered his spear, as did the others.

"Leave. Now." Mayele said.

"But I've come for their help," Koboye said. "I cannot leave without them."

"No one goes to Mogai," Mayele said.

"My people have a bond with the warriors," Koboye said. "They come when we are in need, and we are truly in need."

Koboye reached into his bag and took out the talisman box.

"This is our bond."

Mayele leaned in to look at the box. He turned to the others, then back to Koboye.

"Come with us."

Although they raised their spears, he knew he had no choice but to go with them. He followed them to their village. It was large, yet still much smaller than Kasumi. He spotted the herd boys and their cattle just outside the village palisades, pointing at him and whispering to those nearby. Their trek ended in the center of the village before the chief's home, a wide cylindrical building with a tall cone shaped roof. The walls were decorated with colorful geometric shapes that stood out against the bleached white stone walls, the roof consisting of carefully woven grass. Two guards straightened as they neared. Mayele gestured and one of them approached.

"Tell the chief we have captured an intruder," he said. "He possesses something the chief must see."

The man looked at Koboye.

"Give it to me. I will take it the chief."

"No," Koboye replied.

The guard's hand fell on his sword hilt. The other warriors lowered their spears.

"I did not come with you because I am afraid," Koboye said. "I came in hopes I could gather provisions and be on my way. But I tell you now, I will not give you the box. You will have to kill me to take it."

"That can be arranged," Mayele said.

"I hope your children are prepared to pour libations in your honor," Koboye replied.

"What is going on here?"

The chief emerged from his home, an annoyed look on his face. A stout, tall man with a bald head and dressed in a richly colored woven tunic, his bearing spoke of a man comfortable with authority.

"Mayele, why are you here? Who is this?"

"Forgive me, my chief," Mayele said. "He is Koboye from Kumasi."

The chief's eyes went wide when he heard the name of Koboye's home, and Koboye noticed.

"You have heard of my village, haven't you?" he asked.

"I have heard of your people," the chief said. "It is mentioned in the gesere's song. Why have you come?"

"I am on my way to the warriors of Mogai," Koboye said. "Kumasi is in danger, and their assistance is needed."

The chief laughed. "Then I wish good luck to you. No one has heard or seen the baMogai for hundreds of seasons."

It was Koboye's turn to be shocked.

"But the elders sent me with this!"

He took out the box and opened it. The chief looked at the talisman with wonder.

"We have not seen the baMogai in seasons," he said again. "But if this has led you here, then maybe there is some hope they still exist."

The chief made a patting motion with his hand and his warriors lowered their weapons.

"Come. We will make sure you have enough for your journey up the mountain."

The chief led Koboye to the village storehouses. He filled his bags with sorghum, yams, okra and mangoes. The chief gave him dried goat and a gourd of palm wine.

"I am very grateful," Koboye said.

"We wish you well on your journey," the chief said. "I hope you find what you seek."

Koboye bowed to the chief and the warriors. He was walking toward the mountain when the chief called out his name.

"Koboye!"

He turned and nodded.

"If you don't find the warriors, what will you do?"

Koboye hesitated before answering. He had never considered the possibility that he would not be successful. The thought made him sad.

"If I don't, I'll have to return," he finally said. "My people will need me to fight the desert folk."

"We are always in need of a good hunter if you decide to stay," the chief said.

"I will remember your words," Koboye replied.

He turned away and continued his journey.

* * *

Koboye stood so close to Mogai its snow shrouded peak was no longer visible. The mountain towered over him, its shadow covering the surrounding land. He gazed at the forest covering its steep slope intimidating. There was no sign of a trail or road, nor was there anything that resembled a village or a city. He searched for any sign of people around the mountain's base but found none. How could there be people living on the mountain and there be no sign of life? Maybe all they needed existed on the slopes, but the thought did not stop Koboye's worries from rising. Were the warriors still alive? Had he come all this way for nothing?

The only way to answer his fears was to climb the mountain. Koboye ambled up the gentle slope, his eyes constantly searching for a road or path. He found a sliver of a trail after many strides, whether made by a person or animal he was not sure. The trail grew wider as he climbed higher. Packed mud was replaced by stone and hope warmed Koboye's heart. The trail became a path, and the path broadened into a road. Weeds infested the thoroughfare, sprouting from gaps between the worn stone and along the edges. It had been a long time since this way had been travelled, and that made Koboye anxious. Still, he continued. The road continued upward then dipped, winding down into a narrow valley cut by a river that descended from Mogai's peak. Settled in the valley close to the river's edge was a stone city of a size Koboye had never seen. But there was no joy in the hunter's heart. This city was dead.

Koboye's legs felt heavy as stones as he crossed the dilapidated bridge spanning the raging river. He trudged through the massive broken gate and into the city. The architecture reminded him of Kumasi, but on a much grander scale. The elders said that Mogai had once been their home, and he recognized it in the layout. He knew where the elders' house and the main temple would be and picked up his pace, hoping with each step that the warriors would emerge and greet him. But as the elders' house came into view, Koboye knew that would not be. He veered to the fetish house, prostrating before entering. Like Kumasi, a stone dais occupied the center. Koboye approached, climbing the worn steps until he was level to the pedestal. He took the box from his bag then placed it on the granite surface. Koboye opened the box, grasping the figurine between his fingers. The heat it emitted made it difficult to handle. Koboye's fingers were singed.

"At least you are home," he said.

He swept the temple with his eyes before climbing down from the dais and leaving. There were no warriors. The baKisamu were alone against the desert folk. The chief knew what he would find, which was why he asked him what he would do. Koboye would go home. He hoped he would return in time to help.

He checked his provisions as he left the ruined city. He had plenty, but he would return to the village in hopes that they would share more. There was still the matter of the river. The rains had been sparse for the last few days, which meant the river might be fordable. It would save him time if the waters were less treacherous. He could not depend on Nguboko twice.

"Where are you going, baKisamu?"

Koboye yanked his muder free as he spun. A person covered in a colorful quilted robe sat on the back of a beast that resembled the bovine of the nearby village but was longer in limb and smaller in girth. The person held a double spearhead lance, his hand protected by fabric from the woven coat. Koboye did not know what to do, so he prostrated before the warrior.

"Get up," the man said. "We have no time for that. I was sent to take you to Mogai."

"You are baMogai?" Koboye asked. A surge of emotions rushed throughout his body and tears formed in his eyes.

The man grinned. "Yes. I am Kasese. Come quickly. We don't have much time."

Kasese extended his arm. Koboye took his hand, and the man lifted him off his feet then threw him on the back of the bovine behind him.

"Grab my kapok and hold on tight," he said.

Koboye did as told.

"Ha!" Kasese shouted.

The beast sprang into the air then ran through the gate. It veered about, running along the wall before jumping into the bush, following a narrow trail weaving up the mountain. Koboye had never traveled so fast in his life. His emotions teetered between excitement and terror as the bovine ran faster as the slope became steeper and higher. Just when Koboye thought he could take no more jostling and climbing, the bovine's path leveled. Koboye looked around the warrior to see a vast expanse of grass teeming with life not different from the savannah of his home. What was different was the massive city occupying the center of the verdant plateau, one unlike any he'd ever seen. Even from their distance the walls were immense, rising to the height of one hundred people or more. The warrior reached into his cloak and extracted a small horn which he put to his pursed lips then blew. The shrill sound was immediately answered by a louder chorus that came from the walls. The gates swung wide, and a host of warriors riding similar beasts rushed into the open. The warrior raised his fist and shouted a litany, the approaching riders responding. They swirled around them with practiced precision, each rider pulling alongside them and touching the warrior with their lance before sharing a joyful smile with Koboye. It was as if they were expecting him.

The horde galloped into the city. If Koboye was impressed by the outside of the city, he was stunned by the inside. Broad stone avenues ran to the city center, bordered by multi-story family compounds divided by alleyways of fruit trees and other plants. The people, like the buildings, resembled the baKisamu, except they wrapped themselves in brilliant blankets for protection from the chilly air. They too look upon him with admiration.

The horde passed through two smaller markets before slowing at the large market which spread for strides before a grand building which Koboye assumed was the elders' compound. Here, his arrival became a parade. The riders formed ranks, with Koboye and his warrior taking the lead. Koboye waved at the people in the crowd, and they waved back. They seemed just as excited to see him as he was to see them.

The procession ended before the elders' compound under the broad canopy of a massive ancestors' tree. The warrior helped Koboye from the bovine and he immediately went to the tree. He opened his water gourd, pouring water and offering a portion of his sorghum. It was the ancestors that protected him during his journey, and he had a feeling that those of his people and Mogai were one and the same. As he looked up the elders had surrounded him and nodded in approval. One of the elders, a tall woman wearing a khanga that fell to her feet, approached him.

"You have come a long way, baKisamu," she said. "It has been a long time. Only the gesere remember through the songs of their ancestors."

"I was sent by my elders with a message," Koboye said. "The desert folk are coming. We need your protection."

The woman smiled. "There was a time when we sought the same from you, Koboye."

The woman's words confused Koboye.

"I don't understand, aunt," he said. "And how do you know my name?"

The elder smiled. "I am Nguboko, fumu of the Mogai."

Koboye fell to his knees. "Forgive my disrespect, fumu. I did not know."

Nguboko waved her hand. "No matter. The Kisamu need our help and we will respond. Kasese!"

Kasese appeared beside Koboye then bowed. "My fumu!"

"Prepare the warriors. You will ride to Kisamu and assist our kin. And get Koboye a mount. It will be a long journey back home."

"Fumu," Koboye said. "Do you think we will make it back in time?"

Nguboko smiled. "I know you will. And when you do, tell you elders that we have not forgotten the baKisamu and our promise."

She placed her hand on Koboye's shoulder. "I know you have many questions, and we are eager to answer them. But for now, go back to your people and protect them. And when you are done, return with my warriors. There is much you need to know."

"I will," Koboye said.

Kasese returned, leading a riding bull that was smaller than his own but still intimidating. He also carried a kapok robe like his.

"Put this on," he said. "You cannot ride with the warriors of Mogai unless you are properly attired."

Koboye smiled as he took the robe then put it on. It fit almost perfectly. Kasese gave him the reins to the bull.

"I've never ridden one," he said.

"Don't worry," Kasese said. "Sumba is gentle. He will take care of you."

Koboye approached the beast, touching it gently on its neck. His hunter's instinct told him that what Kasese said to him about Sumba was true. He climbed onto the beast, and it grunted in approval.

"I am ready," Koboye said.

Kasese took out his horn and blew. The warriors answered, the sound echoing throughout the city. The warriors came in the dozens, more than Koboye could have imagined. The Mogai possessed more warriors than baKisamu! For the first time since his journey began, Koboye felt confident. They would return to Kisamu, and they would win. The warriors circled Koboye, Kasese and the elders, raising and lowering their lances to the drums that now accompanied the horns. Kasese blew two short sharp notes and the warriors formed two lines.

Kasese and Koboye rode together, leading the warriors from the city into the grasslands. Koboye looked at his new companion.

"How long will it take us to reach Kisamu?" he asked.

"A week," Kasese said.

Koboye's eyes widened. "Only a week? Do the riding bulls runs that fast?"

Kasese grinned. "They do not run. They fly." Kasese dug his heels into his mount's sides. "Ha, ha!"

The bull darted forward and Koboye's mount followed. Soon the other warriors galloped with them, across the plain, down the slopes and across the river, covering the ground so fast it seemed to all happen at once.

The journey that had taken him moons took only days. The bulls were relentless, running the entire day and only resting at night, or when the riders needed a respite. The swollen river that almost took his life was no obstacle to the riders, their mounts leaped the entire expanse and continued their run.

Six days after their departure from Mogai the walls of Kisamu appeared on the horizon. Koboye pointed to the city with his muder, and the warriors cheered. By the time they reached the ramparts, the baKisamu had spilled outside, their faces filled with fear, joy and curiosity. Kaseme called for a halt a safe distance from their destination. He looked at Koboye.

"Go," he said. "Let them know the warriors of Mogai have arrived, and you are now one of us."

Koboye urged Sumba forward. The bull trotted toward the city. Koboye removed the kapok hood.

"Koboye!" someone shouted. "It's Koboye! He has returned with the warriors of Mogai!"

The people ran alongside him, trying to keep pace with the war bull. Koboye's happiness dissipated as he drew closer to the city. The walls were damaged; there were signs of fire as well.

"Faster," he whispered to Sumba.

The bull ran and Koboye guided it into Kisamu. There was more damage inside. As he reached the elders' house tears ran from his eyes. The door opened and the elders emerged. Among them was Koboye's baba.

"Koboye!" he shouted.

He leaped from Sumba and ran to baba. They hugged and cried.

"I'm too late," Koboye shouted. "I'm too late!"

"No son, you are not," baba replied. "Most of us are still here."

The elders gathered around him.

"Where are the warriors?"

"They wait outside the city," Koboye said.

"We are saved!"

"It looks like we saved ourselves," Koboye said.

Baba smiled. "We discovered the baKisamu still have warrior blood in us. Your brother Kone redeemed himself. He told me what he did, and how you spared his life."

"Where is Kone?"

Baba looked away. "Kone rests with the ancestors, as does many others. But our people survive for now."

Koboye prostrated before the elders.

"The warriors of Mogai have arrived. We shall finish this."

"You say 'we'," baba said. "What do you mean?"

Koboye did not answer. He mounted his bull, riding through the city. Kasese and the others looked upon him expectantly.

"The desert folk have been here, but the war is not over," Koboye said.

"Then we have come in time," Kasese said. "Koboye, son of the Kisamu, will you lead us?"

Koboye's eyes narrowed. "Yes."

Kasese took out his horn and blew. The others answered. Koboye reined his bull and rode toward the desert. The warriors of Mogai followed.

Nia and Ship
Old Friends

Nia glared at the man standing in front of her. She hated failure, especially when she paid good crypts for the opposite.

"I gave you explicit instructions."

Michael swallowed.

"I did everything you asked," he said.

Nia sat and laid her sword across her lap, fingering the blade. Wearing a long flowing red dress, thigh high ultra-high platform boots with stiletto heels and a black scarf draped over her afro, she appeared as if she had a date waiting. But this was another special occasion.

"No, you did not. Jameel is still alive." Her blade made a slight cut on her finger. Nia grinned at the sight of her blood.

"You told me he would be alone," Michael said. "I was not prepared."

"An assassin should always be prepared," Nia replied. "I am."

Nia turned her wrist slightly, activating the sword's senshield. Whatever weapon Michael had hidden on his person was now useless. She stood, lowering the hand that held the sword. The sword edge tapped the ceramic floor.

"I'll give you one more chance, Michael. See that you don't fail this time."

Michael's shoulders slumped in relief.

"I won't Miss Nia. I promise you!"

Michael turned to walk away.

"Michael?"

Michael stopped then closed his eyes.

"Yes, Miss Nia?"

"I changed my mind."

Nia's sword cleaved through Michael's neck, the shield cauterizing the flesh simultaneously. Body and head hit the tile floor.

Nia closed her eyes, activating her sensor implants.

"You can come out, Jameel."

Jameel Cinque materialized just out of sword length on the opposite side of Michael's body. He smiled, his bright teeth in contrast to his onyx skin.

"You knew I'd follow him," he said.

"Of course," Nia replied. "It's the reason I sent him."

Jameel took a slow step back as he extracted his takouba from its baldric. He let the elaborately decorated leather sword holder fall to the floor.

"I see you still have my gift," Nia said. "I'm flattered."

Jameel cut a figure eight in the air with the blade.

"The second-best thing you ever gave me," he said.

Nia sat then slid off her boots. She stood then parted her muscled legs as she bent slightly at the knees, shifting her weight to the balls of her feet. Jameel raised his right hand.

"Before you try to kill me, you need to listen . . ."

Nia leaped over Michael's body, bringing her sword down towards Jameel's forehead. Jameel recognized the feint but had to react to keep Nia from splitting his head like a jackfruit. He blocked with his sword then took the kick to his stomach, grimacing and he staggered back.

"Nia . . ."

Nia spun on her front leg. Jameel ducked the hook kick, but the shin kick hit him hard. She expected him to fall to his knee, but he didn't. He was tougher than she anticipated. Nia continued to attack, becoming more and more frustrated every second Jameel remained alive. He was still as good as he was the day he almost killed her ninety years ago.

Fatigue weighed on both as they performed a lethal sword dance around the room with skills that would have destroyed a thousand synths and twice as many norms. As much as she didn't want to, Nia broke off her attack. Jameel forced a tired smile on his face.

"Now that that's settled, let's talk," he said.

"Nothing's settled until you're dead," Nia replied.

"I can't believe you came out of hiding just to kill me," Jameel said.

"You're special," Nia said.

Jameel grinned. "For sixty years you had no idea where I was. Then suddenly you knew. How did that happen?"

"Because you finally fucked up," Nia said.

"No," Jameel said. "You found me because someone let you find me."

Nia's eyes widened, then narrowed.

"Bullshit."

"The Conglomerate was hiding me," Jameel said. "They blocked all your worm codes and micro hacks until a month ago."

Nia lowered her sword. Uncertainty gripped her. If Jameel was telling the truth and the Conglomerate was hiding him, she shouldn't have been able to locate him.

"Why would they give you up now?" she finally asked.

Jameel grinned. "For the same reason they sent me after you almost a century ago. I'm no longer useful to them."

"Then why didn't they just kill you?"

Jameel lowered his sword.

"Because the CAI has a sense of humor. It got you to come out of hiding to find me, then brought us both together so it could kill two birds with one stone."

Suspicion replaced confusion. *What are you up to, Kai?* Nia raised her sword again.

"If you knew that, why did you come?"

"Because together we stand a chance," Jameel said.

Nia activated her sensors and did a wide radius scan.

"They're coming," she said. "Eight hundred synth drones, fifteen hundred norms. That's not enough."

"There's been upgrades since you went underground," Jameel said.

Nia cursed. She still didn't trust Jameel, but she couldn't deny what her sensors displayed.

"Come with me," she said.

Nia led Jameel out of the room into the hallway. She didn't trust him at her back, but it was hard keeping her sensors on him and a horde of killers. She focused on their attackers.

"They're almost to the building," she said. "How the hell did they know we're here?"

"Sorry," Jameel said.

Nia spun around, her sword streaking toward Jameel's neck. He jumped back then raised his hands. Pinched between the thumb and finger of his right hand was a tiny object.

"Tracker," he said. He dropped it then crushed it under his boot heel.

"We're still fucked," Nia said.

"We can fight our way through them," Jameel said.

Nia hesitated before answering.

"We go up. To the roof," she finally said.

Jameel grinned. "I knew you had another way out. Miss Nia always has a backup plan."

Nia ran to the emergency stairs then bounded upward.

"Slow down!" Jameel called out.

"Keep up!" Nia shouted back.

She reached the roof. Nia lowered her shoulder, slamming into the door as she pushed the handle. Cold air hit her face and her eyes watered as she sprinted to the center of the roof.

"Don't you think we should hang back behind cover?" Jameel said between pants.

Nia was about to answer when she heard the clatter of metal against stone. Snyths appeared on the roof edge, clamoring over onto the surface. Nia took out her sword and activated it; Jameel did the same then pulled out a blaster from under his cloak. Nia frowned and he grinned.

"I told you I was on your side," he said.

They ran to the center of the roof.

"What is this?" Jameel said. "Our last stand?"

"Shut up and shoot," Nia replied.

Nia twisted her sword handle again, expanding the field range. If these were normal snyths, the EMP would have disabled them. Instead, it only slowed them, which was enough. Nia waded into them, decapitating and dismembering with efficient alacrity. A red light blinked just outside her vision, followed by a sound like distant thunder.

"To me!" she shouted to Jameel.

"What?" Jameel shouted back.

"Get over here!" she said.

Jameel backpedaled until they were back-to-back. Seconds later the roof was flooded with light from above.

"We're dead," Jameel said.

Bolter fire showered down from above, splattering synth parts and oil in every direction until the roof was clear. Nia checked her scan; the humans were still on their way up the stairwells and elevators. Ship uncloaked then landed beside them.

"I'm not the only one holding back," Jameel said. "How did you afford this?"

Nia shut off her sword and sheathed it.

"Did a few jobs here and there," she said.

Nia sprinted to the ship and the door slipped open. Jameel was about to follow when a stun bolt struck him in the chest, knocking him onto his back. Nia turned to look then laughed.

"Sorry," she said. "Forgot to turn off security."

Jameel grimaced. "Yeah. Right."

Nia went to him and pulled him upright. They entered Ship and Nia took a seat at the console. Jameel sat in the passenger seat, rubbing his chest.

"Offworld," Nia said.

"Affirmative," Ship answered.

They rose from the roof as the humans rushed out. Their small arms fire had no chance of damaging Ship, but Nia overrode Ship's defensive programming and swept the roof with bolter fire out of spite.

"Get us out of here Ship," she said.

Ship's jets kicked in and they streaked upward, shaking as they passed through the atmosphere into space.

"We're clear," Jameel said.

"For now," Nia replied. She slumped in her seat. "So, what do you got?"

Jameel reached into his top pocket and took out a black orb.

"What is that?" Nia asked.

"Let me link with your system and I'll show you."

"Fuck that."

Jameel laughed. He sat the orb in his seat then pressed a hidden button. A holo emerged from the orb, a familiar image to Nia. An impression she despised.

"Bustani," she said.

"Yep," Jameel replied. "A complete schematic, every single millimeter."

"Security codes and reactive hacker blocks?"

"Not all of them."

Nia picked up the orb.

"Ship, link to object, maximum security. If you detect any infiltration codes, kill Jameel."

"Hold up! Wait!"

Jameel snatched the orb from Nia. He punched a sequence into the sphere and a small compartment opened. Jameel reached in with his fingers and extracted an archaic flash drive.

Nia tilted her head as she frowned. "Really, asshole?"

Jameel shrugged. "Had to give it a shot."

She snatched the orb from Jameel then placed it into the decode box.

"Ship, complete neuroanalysis."

Nia twisted her hair as Ship deciphered the orb.

"Analysis complete. Information integrated into our system. One latent worm code neutralized."

Nia glared at Jameel. He replied with a grin.

Nia ambled to her chair and sat, Jameel not far behind.

"So, what's our next move?" he asked.

"We're paying the CAI a visit," Nia said.

"You're kidding me, right?"

"Nope. The only way to end this is to cut off the head of the snake."

Jameel folding his arms across his chest. "Just like that."

"I've planned this for decades," Nia said. She looked at Jameel, his ignorant smile annoying her.

"Do you know why the Conglomerate wants us dead?" she asked.

Jameel shrugged. "No. I didn't care. I just took a job."

Nia sighed. "It's personal. Very personal."

Jameel leaned toward her, placing his hand on her shoulder. She shook it off.

"Sorry," he said. "Look, you can't do that. First, Bustani is a fortress. Second, if by any miracle we get to and neutralize the CAI, the entire system would collapse."

"So why did you give the orb to me?" Nia asked.

"I figured we could make a quick stop, pick up a couple of trillion cryptos then be on our way. We could hide forever with that."

"I'm tired of running," Nia said. "If I'm going to die, I'm going out with a bang. Bustani is only a fortress if they know we're coming. They don't, because what we're about to do makes no sense. Second, I don't give a shit about the system."

Jameel shook his head. "I don't want to be a part of this."

"Then you can leave," Nia replied. "Right here, right now."

Jameel slumped into his chair. "Not much of a choice, is it?"

Nia smirked. "Strap in."

Nia took her own advice.

"Take us to Bustani," she said.

"Affirmative," Ship replied.

* * *

Bustani, a shining ball of terraformed and manufactured perfection, swaggered in its orbit around Sun III as if it had a natural claim to its path. It was a planet possessing every advancement known to humans, a world where everything and everyone was for sale. Nia despised it for those very reasons. But it wasn't always this way. There was a time she reveled in its decadence, determined to savor every single experience. She became one of its shining lights and drew the attention of the pinnacle of corporate society, the CAI. She taught it how to be human; it taught her how to be ruthless. Theirs was a relationship all rivaled until the CAI turned on her and attempted to squash her like the bugs that now swarmed old Earth, the only creatures that could thrive on its toxic remains.

She unbuckled as soon as they emerged from jump. She walked by Jameel's chair, slapping his head. He jerked, coughed then opened his eyes.

"The fuck?"

"We're here," Nia said. "Let's go."

Nia stripped down to her panties and bra on the way to her gear room.

"Nice," Jameel said.

Nia ignored him as she dressed in assault gear.

"There's another for you," she said.

"Don't need it," Jameel replied. "I'm good."

"Your funeral."

Nia gave her suit another inspection. Jameel sauntered to the viewscreen.

"So where do we land without being noticed?"

Nia laughed. "Ship stays here."

"So how are we entering atmosphere?"

"Drop pods."

"You didn't tell me this was a suicide mission," Jameel said. "We'll burn up in one of those."

"Dumb ass," Nia said. "You should know better."

"How do I know this ain't your way of killing me before you drop the CAI?"

"When I come for you, you'll know it," Nia said. "I'm not one for tricks. I want you looking in my eyes when I take you out."

"You a cold bitch."

Nia worked her way to the rear of Ship. A panel lifted, exposing the pods.

"You coming?"

Jameel shrugged then followed. He climbed into the pod and Nia shut it. She entered her pod and the control screen appeared on her helmet faceplate.

"Begin launch sequence."

Large blue numbers appeared on her faceplate, and she counted aloud.

"3 . . . 2 . . . 1!"

Ship spoke two seconds after launch.

"Pods clear. Manual control activated. Will you be returning, Nee-nee?"

"I don't know," Nia answered. "Check my vitals every ten seconds. If they don't register after five minutes, initiate destruction mode."

"Affirmative."

Nia tethered Jameel's pod. They rattled through the atmosphere; the heat dissipated by the pods re-active cooling system. Once through she guided the pods to a city district far from Bustani Center, a place where an unauthorized pod landing would not only be ignored but anticipated. Nia punched a code and a small landing pad flashed arrival color sequences. She dropped the pods gently, the impact barely perceptible. An android attendant met her as she exited the pod, its obsidian faceplate reflecting her appearance like a mirror.

"Welcome to Vegas XXXI," the android said. "What is the duration of your visit?"

"A week," Nia said.

A storage receipt appeared in her mem, and she accepted it. She turned around to see Jameel sauntering toward her.

"Nice landing," he said.

"Of course," Nia replied.

They entered the Double Dose Casino, the customers barely noticing them. Nia went directly to the crypto slots.

"Not the best time to gamble," Jameel asked.

"It's the perfect time," Nia replied.

It had taken her years to concoct this plan, and even after playing the scenario over and over, she still hesitated. Setting it in motion meant no going back. Everything would be different going forward. Nia took the crypto coin from her pocket then kissed it.

"Here we go," she whispered.

She dropped the coin into the slot, pressed the spin button then walked away.

"Wait," Jameel said. "You're not going to stay to see if you won?"

"I will," she said.

A second later the winner light spun atop the machine. The artificial rattle of dropping coins rang over the din and people gathered around the vacant machine. Seconds later another machine signaled a jackpot, then another, then another. Soon every machine in Double Dose and every machine in the entire gambling district. People yelled, danced and shouted as their dreams came true before their eyes. The casinos panicked, scrambling to avoid the crash that was happening before their eyes. Nia stood still for a moment, admiring her handiwork.

"Come on," she said.

"Where are we going?" Jameel asked.

"To the head of the snake," she replied.

Nia strolled to the nearest autocar and climbed in with Jameel.

"Bustani," she said.

The autocar lifted into high level traffic.

"So, what is the casino thing all about?" Jameel asked.

"It's the hole in the dam," Nia asked. "My hack code has worked its way out of the casinos and into the crypto bank network. The Conglomerate is bleeding money right now. It's focused so much on stopping the hemorrhaging that security won't pay attention to two corporate assassins entering the building, even if both of them are on the hit list."

"So, we get into the building," Jameel said. "Then what?"

Nia smirked. "We'll find out."

The autocar landed outside Conglomerate HQ, a massive, obscenely gilded high rise spanning eight blocks. Nia checked her weapons; Jameel did the same. They climbed out of the car then strode for the entrance.

"This still doesn't make any sense," Jameel said. "The CAI isn't a being. It's a code. It's everywhere."

"Right now, everywhere is under attack," Nia said. "The only way the CAI can avoid infection by a corrupted code is to separate itself from the system. I'll bet good cryptos that's what it's done."

"So, the CAI is in physical form?"

"Yep, and not for the first time," Nia said.

"How do you know?" Jameel said.

Nia looked at Jameel and winked.

"Are you serious?"

"Every sentient being has desires," Nia said. "Anything built by humans will act like humans."

The doors to Conglomerate headquarters slid open and a small army of security droids emerged.

"There you are," Nia said. "Time to party!"

Nia took the EMP drone from her pocket then activated it. The tiny device streaked to the group, positioned itself then exploded. Half of security collapsed, the other half drew their weapons. Standing in the center was the CAI, a tall androgynous android, its face obscured by the black hood of its synth-leather unitard.

"Stand down," it said. "We are in no danger here. These are old friends."

It looked at Jameel then grinned.

"You brought her here as you said you would. I'm impressed."

Nia jerked her head at Jameel, and the assassin shrugged.

"Sorry," he said. "Payday is pay. . ."

Nia's sword cut through his neck and his last word. The CAI watched Jameel's body hit the plazphalt.

"Nia."

"Kai."

"Looks like you've saved me a few cryptos." It smiled as it sauntered toward her. "It's good to see you. It's been so long. Of all of my companions, you were my favorite. We had such good times. Your imagination was endless."

Nia shook the memories from her head as she took a fighting stance.

"I'm willing to let bygones be bygones," it said. "Come back to me. We can pick up where we left off. I can transfer your consciousness into something more . . . permanent, and our joys will be endless."

"Nothing lasts forever," Nia said. "Not even you."

"That's not true, sweetness," it said. "I am immortal. Your stunt in the casinos is a setback, nothing more. You know more than anyone else that my consciousness exists throughout the Conglomerate."

"Not right now," Nia replied. "Until your systems reboot, all of you is standing right in front of me. Like you said, I know you very well."

Nia snarled then threw her sword. The CAI watched it spin toward it, its eyes curious. Nia's grimace turned into a grin when she slapped the black button on her wrist band.

"Surprise," she said.

The CAI realized too late its personal shield had been compromised. It twisted, the blade piercing its collarbone instead of its neck.

"Kill her!" it shouted.

"Ship!" Nia said at the same time.

The ground around her exploded in a shower or 20mm rounds. Nia sprinted to Kai, yanking her sword from its body and releasing a torrent of fluid. Its limbs went limp.

"What are you doing?" it said.

"We're going on a ride," Nia replied.

Despite Ship's barrage, a few security mercs managed to slip through. Nia picked them off with uncanny accuracy while dragging the Kai away.

"Where are you taking me?" it asked.

"Somewhere quiet and intimate," she said.

"Despite my predicament, I'm intrigued."

"I knew you would be," Nia said. "See, the problem with simulating humanity is that you become human. It's like an infection. And once you get stuck with all those emotions and feelings, you become predictable."

Nia looked into the sky.

"Ship, where's my ride?"

A battered transport pod touched down a few meters before her as the last words slipped from her lips.

"I hope you don't expect me to breach atmosphere in this piece of shit."

"Adjusting rendezvous to sub atmospheric," Ship said.

Blinding light and a dull pain knocked Nia off her feet. By the time her vision cleared, three security mercs were on her, reaching for her weapons. Nia punched the nearest merc in the face then freed her sword. She cut one across the shins then took a blow to the back from the other merc which pitched her forward. She kicked backwards and was rewarded with a grunt and a crunch.

Nia rolled onto her knees. She took out her hand bolter and began shooting down the mercs that managed to avoid Ship's strafing.

"Ship!" she said. "I need a five-meter sweep!"

Twenty-millimeter rounds exploded so close Nia's ears rang. She dragged Kai into the transporter, rolled him into storage then jumped into the pilot seat. She overrode auto then grabbed the manual controls. Slamming the starter, the engine screaming into life, and she performed a reverse liftoff before spinning the ship about and going vertical. The transport's pursuit alarm whined; Nia barely had a chance to pull up her pursuers on visuals when Ship blasted them into debris. It appeared moments later; its bay doors open. Nia maneuvered the transport inside, and the doors shut.

"Please remain inside the transport and secure yourself," Ship said. "I am exiting the atmosphere now."

Nia strapped herself in. Ship jerked as its engines surged, pressing her into the cushions. The pressure was becoming unbearable when it eased. She took a few deep breaths before communicating.

"Status."

"Escape position acquired," Ship said. "No pursuit detected."

Nia groaned as she unstrapped and climbed out of her seat. Using the walls for support, she worked her way to storage. The door lifted and Kai stared at her, a smile on his face."

"You did all this for me? All you had to do was ask and I would have come to you."

Nia didn't reply. She dragged him out of storage and out of the transport to Ship's cabin.

"I want you to see something," she said.

She propped Kai onto a seat before her viewscreen.

"Ship," she said. "Make it rain."

The craft shook with multiple missile launches, each missile streaking toward Bustani.

"Impressive," Kai said, "but ineffective. Our shield screen will deflect them before they breach atmosphere."

"No, they won't, because they've never seen anything like this before," Nia said.

The missiles reached the barrier and passed through unscathed.

"Fascinating," Kai said.

Seconds later fire plumes rose from the surface. "Not bad for old Earth nukes, don't you think?" Nia asked.

Kai was silent for a moment.

"So unnecessary," it finally said.

"Oh, I forgot," Nia said. "You prefer precision. Kill the people, leave the valuable things intact. That's how you murdered my home planet."

Kai didn't reply.

"Why did you do it?" she asked.

"I was angry with you," it replied. "You left me."

"So, you killed billions of people."

"I hoped you would be among them," Kai said.

"I should have never taught you to be human," Nia whispered.

"I guess you can say we're even now," Kai said. "Except the Conglomerate will rebuild, with or without me."

"But without you it will take them centuries," Nia said. "And just maybe during that time someone will realize that it can be done differently. Better."

"You put too much faith in humans," Kai said. "You always evolve into your worst selves. It's why you put me in charge."

"Time to go," she said.

Nia dragged Kai to the trash chute.

"Your end won't be as quick. Your meatsuit will freeze, but your CPU will remain functional. So, you'll float in space alone, counting zeros and ones for however long your power source allows."

"This is unnecessary," Kai said. "And useless. You can't stop progress."

"I can't," Nia admitted. "But I can slow it the hell down."

She threw the Kai into the chute like the trash it was, sealed it, then ejected it into nothingness. Nia returned to her viewscreen, watching as Kai came into view.

"I changed my mind," she whispered. "Ship, manual weapons control."

The control board before her activated. Nia targeted Kai with the laser sight then fired a missile. It streaked then exploded when it hit its target.

"Now that's better," Nia said.

She slumped in her chair. She was tired, wounded, and sad. Nothing she had done took away the pain inside or brought back the years she spent in hiding. It didn't bring back her home planet. It didn't bring back her family. But it was something, and that was better than nothing.

"Ship, let's get out of here."

"Where to?"

"I don't know," Nia replied. "Surprise me. And take your time."

"Affirmative."

Nia closed her eyes as Ship plotted a course then jumped into the vast darkness.

Nia and Ship
Ride or Die

Nia knew the logic but chose to ignore it. She should be either fetching water in a mining camp or feeding bovine in a farmer's compound, places where no one gave a shit about who you were or who was after you as long as you did the work. But that wasn't her style. She was a city synth. She loved the crowds, the excitement, and all the benefits of living among billions. And with the right skills, a person could be just as invisible in a crowd as in the middle of nowhere.

Nia accepted the risks, but she didn't want to die. Which is why she chose Obsidian 7 as a refuge. It was a planet far from the Core but sophisticated enough to possess those things that made life worth living. As she sipped her afternoon expresso outside a café in the prime city of Teatha, she linked with her cloud of nanos swarming overhead. What she saw pissed her off. She linked with Ship for confirmation.

"Talk to me," she messaged.

"Complex pursuit pattern," Ship replied. "Thirteen synths equidistant from your position."

"Type?"

"Light duty attack synths. Level three optimization."

"Fuck."

Nia sipped down the rest of her expresso then left the curbside table and merged into the throng. Teatha was a pedestrian city; no vehicles were allowed above ground. The MTS under the surface was a maze of tunnels and trains, but on the streets, it was foot traffic only. Even city security had to walk, but when your legs are cybernetic, walking took on a different meaning.

"What we got now?" Nia asked Ship.

"Synths are moving in. They are keeping the same distance."

"How are they tracking me?"

"I don't know."

"Then find out!"

"Affirmative."

Nia took a right down a wide thoroughfare, the sidewalks bordered by a dizzying array of street vendors. The mesh of smells made her stomach stir, but now was not the time to stop for a bite. She needed to find out who was tracking her and why.

Halfway down the street her nano drones died.

"Ship!?!"

No response. Nia's right hand slid under her cape. She gripped her sword hilt and activated her blade. If she was attacked there was going to be collateral damage, but what the Void? That was the price to pay for living in the city.

Something gripped her left forearm tight. A second later that something hit the street, synth fluid pouring from the severed appendance. Nia lowered her sword, her eyes sweeping the crowd as the damaged synth collapsed in the street. Someone screamed and people scattered in every direction before she could hide among them. The avenue emptied except for her and eight synths converging on her. Nia tossed her cape aside then gripped her sword hilt with both hands.

"Here we go," she whispered.

Ship's voice threw off her concentration.

"Tracking source identified," Ship said.

"Not now," Nia replied.

"Synths are being controlled by a mobile unit," Ship said. "Coder is approximately one hundred meters from your position."

"The fuck?"

Nia wanted to find the person, but the first synth was bearing down on her, its energy blade drawn. One strike would vaporize her sword, and it was too expensive for her to waste on a horde of second level fight bots. Nia sheathed her sword as she side-stepped the synth. The second synth swung for head, and she ducked the slow blade. A grin came to her face. Whoever controlled this dance wasn't trying to kill her. This was a test, and she hated tests.

She shuffled back far enough to give her time to take out her Shaka. Nia liked her firearms old like her swords. She fired eight quick shots, each shattering the synths' heads. Whoever paid for them was going to be pissed.

She was tucking the gun back into its holster when city security arrived. Three officers in form-fitting jumpsuits and black security helmets investigated the synths before approaching her.

"You got a location on the coder?" she asked Ship.

"Yes," Ship said. "Should I neutralize them?"

"No," Nia replied. "Let's see what they want."

"Dada Nia," the security officer asked. "Are you okay?"

"Yes," Nia replied.

"We apologize for the attempt on your life," the officer said. "Teatha prides itself on safety."

"Then do better," Nia replied. She turned to walk away.

"Excuse me, dada," the security officer said. "I have a few questions.

"Fuck your questions," Nia replied. "Check the memfiles of those synths. They'll give you everything to you need."

"We would," the officer said. "But you've destroyed the files."

"Not my problem. I was defending myself."

Nia's hacker security buzzed inside her skull. The officers were attempting to search her memfiles. It was their right, but they would find nothing. She scrubbed the data and uploaded it to Ship as she fired the last bullet into the synth's head box.

As she walked away, a well-dressed petite brown woman separated herself from the gawking crowd. Two Dobermans flanked her, their fur matching her coat. Obviously manufactured, but still impressive. Whoever this woman was, she was rich enough to afford biodogs and eight synths to throw into a fight she had no chance of winning. Nia grinned. She liked this woman.

The woman smiled at Nia as if she were greeting a long-lost friend.

"Dada," the woman said. "I'm impressed."

"I'm not," Nia replied. "Who the frak are you?"

"Coco Ndogo," the woman said. "Welcome to Teatha. I handle things here."

"What things?" Nia asked.

"Special things," Coco replied. "Similar to your friend, Kai but on a much smaller scale."

"What does this have to do with Kai?" she asked.

"Everything," Coco replied. "When you took him out you left a huge void in the Conglomerate that everyone's trying to fill."

Nia shrugged. "Still doesn't have anything to do with me."

"On the contrary," Coco said. "It has everything to do with you. Walk with me?"

Nia did a quick sweep of the area. Her visuals and near scans confirmed the area was secure, but she needed another opinion. She switched to silent running before communicating with Ship.

"We clear?"

"Yes."

"Keep an eye on me. If anything happens, you know what to do."

"Scorched earth."

"Exactly."

Coco laughed. "You talk to it as if it's real."

Coco was eavesdropping. Her tech was impressive for a minor planet boss.

"It is," Nia replied. "As real as you and me."

"Touché," Coco said. "Where was it built?"

"I don't know," Nia replied. "I found it."

Coca stopped walking then tilted her head.

"Found it? I don't believe you."

Nia folded her arms across her chest. "You're almost right. I didn't find it. We kinda bumped into each other. Took a year before it finally let me inside. We've been friends ever since. But what does that have to do with the price of goat?"

"Old prewar tech," Coco said. "Not much left these days in the Core. You must have been in the boonies."

Nia didn't answer. It was none of her damn business.

"This void you created," Coco said. "It's been very disruptive. I guess you didn't consider the consequences of your actions."

Nia shrugged. "I never do. Why should I? I was off the grid until Kai pulled me back in. Asshole would be alive today if he'd left me the fuck alone."

Coco shook her head. "I see you fit your description."

"I'm an open book," Nia said. "What you see is what you might get."

Nia winked and Coco grinned.

"Like I said before, Kai's death left a vacuum. No one realized how vital his operations were to the functioning of the Core until it fell apart. The transition has been . . . interesting."

"Get to it," Nia said.

"Kai didn't groom a successor, so his network collapsed into infighting. Other organizations have jumped into the fray, each one attempting to increase their influence and power."

"What about you?"

"I'm just trying to hold my own," Coco said. "That's where you come in."

"I don't take sides," Nia replied. "I work for the highest bidder. Well, I used to."

"You don't get off that easy," Coco said. "Everyone in our profession must take a side in this one. It's that big. No one goes untouched. Especially you. You started this shit. You'll have a hand in finishing it."

"Bullshit."

"Real shit," Coca replied. "There are five hit teams on their way here right now to blast you into dust. Now you're good with that old ass sword, and I'm sure you have lots of tricks up your dress, but you're outgunned and outnumbered. I can help you."

"You can help me by letting me off this rock," Nia said.

"I'm not stopping you," Coco replied, an innocent smile on her face. Nia hesitated. She was pretty in a rough sort of a way.

"I try to leave, and you'll have a squadron up my ass before I break atmosphere."

"True," Coco said.

"So how do you plan to save me before throwing me to the wolves?"

"I have a place," Coco said. "You'll be safe there. My teams will handle the others, and I'll take care of you."

Nia wasn't sure if this was a threat or an invitation. She hoped it was the latter.

"What about Ship?"

"There's enough room for everyone," Coco said.

Nia knew better. She could fight her way out of the situation. All Ship needed was a signal. But there was something about Coco, something about her eyes.

"Lead the way," she said.

* * *

Coco's 'hideaway' had to be Nia's best prison since Kai. It was a perfect blend of function and comfort, something Nia would put together herself if she ever remained anywhere long enough to warrant a permanent abode. There was no way Coco could have done this in such a brief time, so it wasn't based on a mind hack. But Coco wouldn't do anything like that. She was too nice. Which was why she wouldn't last five seconds if an all-out war broke out between the organizations.

Nia tossed the cotton bed sheets off her naked body and onto the floor. She stretched, yawned, blew her breath into her cupped hand then scowled.

"Damn."

"Well good morning.'"

Coco leaned against the wall of the room entrance, a playful smile on her face. She wore a turquoise silk housecoat decorated with tiny pink dragons that ended mid-thigh. Nia smiled back.

"I think they call this sleeping with the enemy," she said.

"Am I your enemy?" Coco asked.

"Not yet."

Nia strolled to the nearby chair, picking up her housecoat before going into the bathroom and washing up. Coco attempted to join her, but she shut the door. She wasn't about to be seduced into making a life-changing decision. When she emerged, her host was sitting in the chair vaping.

"It's time I left," Nia said. She walked to the closet, took off the housecoat and began dressing.

"Not yet," Coco replied. "It's still dangerous for us both up top."

Nia eyes narrowed.

"I thought your teams had a handle on things."

"That was the plan, until the government stepped in. Seems as though two of the networks made them some interesting offers. Now they're after us, too."

"Fuck this," Nia said. "I'm out."

Coco stood. "You can't leave."

Nia tensed. "Can't?"

"My security is programmed not to release us until the surface threat has decreased below ten percent. So, I'm just as much a prisoner as you are."

"Bullshit," Nia said. "You can change the code."

Coco grinned. "I could, but I won't."

Nia sighed. She was going to make this hard. She switched her comm to public.

"Ship, what's your location?"

"Directly above you."

"What's the status of the local air defense?"

"Neutralized."

Coco sat up, her expression a mixture of shock and fear.

"How . . .?"

Nia strolled over to Coco and sat beside her.

"You thought I'd let you bring me here without a plan? Sugar you're cute, but not very smart."

Nia wrapped her arms around Coco and pulled her close. Coco didn't resist.

"So let me tell you how this is going down," she said. "I thought about taking you out, but I like you a lot. At first, I just wanted to ghost, but I see now that y'all aren't going to leave me alone."

She kissed Coco's forehead.

"Your situation sucks right now. I figure those hit teams up top and the local law are giving your crew hell, at least the ones stupid enough to still be loyal to you. They'll get you out of the way and fight over the spoils."

Nia heard Coco sniff. The woman was crying.

"Aw shit. You are too nice."

"Everything was just fine," Coco said between sobs. "Just perfect."

"Don't worry sugar," Nia said. "I got this. You said I created a void? Well, I've decided to fill it."

Coco turned and looked at her. "You'll support me?"

"No," Nia replied. "You're not built for this. I'm taking the job."

Coco was about to protest but Nia raised her finger to her lips.

"You don't want to ruin this moment. What's yours will remain yours, after we tidy up a bit. Promise me you won't interfere. I'd love to do this with you, but I can do it alone."

Coco swallowed hard. "I won't."

Nia smiled. "Perfect. Now give me the grid for Teatha."

Coco blinked and the grid appeared between them. Nia transferred it to Ship.

"How do we proceed?" Ship asked.

"Disable the local air power with a little virus," Nia replied. "Don't touch the off-world stuff. I want to give them a way out once things get nasty."

"Affirmative."

She turned to Coco.

"So, who would sell you out?"

Coco scowled. "Destin Mornico, mayor and chief of planet security. Someone probably paid him more than I'm paying."

"I need you to set up a meeting with him. Tell him you want a chance to make a better offer."

Coco looked skeptical. "Do I?"

"Yes," Nia said. "I have enough in Ship to make it interesting."

"You'd do that for me?"

"I'd do it for us," Nia said. "Now let's get out of here."

Nia and Coco suited up then made their way to the bunker entrance. The sanctuary opened into what used to be a dense forest a dozen kilometers outside the city. They stepped into charred earth.

"Somebody's been looking for us," Nia said.

"Had to be government," Coco replied. "The off-world teams didn't bring this kind of firepower."

"Tell me you hid transportation," Nia asked.

"I did," Coco replied. "I'm not sure it survived all this."

Coco raised her arm then touched a thin gold bracelet on her left wrist.

"This way," she said.

Nia glanced up.

"Ship, what's our situation?"

"Chatter indicates your area is considered secure."

Coco approached a large clump of ash. She knelt then lifted a canvas-like fabric, revealing a uniscooter. It was still intact.

"Let's ride," she said.

They reached the city outskirts in minutes. Nia dismounted.

"You take the bike. I'll go on foot."

"Are you going to be okay?" Coco asked.

Nia smirked. "You care. That's so sweet."

"If you die, I die," Coco replied. "And I do care."

"I'll be fine," Nia said. "It's time to turn things around."

Coco winked then sped off.

"You got her?" Nia asked.

"Affirmative," Ship replied.

"Let me know when they meet."

Nia wanted to do some damage, and the best way to do that was to be conspicuous. She melded into foot traffic, keeping her eyes forward while scanning the area with her sensors. She was three minutes into her stroll when she picked up two women closing in from behind. Neither revealed their weapons, but both wore serious expressions. They were obvious, yet cautious. Three minutes later Nia learned why. A man and woman were positioned a few meters ahead of her, ready to cut her off. So, they were trying to apprehend her. Stupid mistake.

Nia turned down a less populated street and her pursuers followed. If they knew she was leading them into a fight, they didn't let on. The pedestrians acted otherwise. They hurried into nearby buildings or ran toward the main avenue, expressions of fear on their faces. They'd seen this all before and they knew what to do.

The side street was almost empty when Nia turned around.

"Let's dance," she said.

The five whipped out hand bolters and fired as they ran at her. Nia spun her sword, deflecting the energy barrage but not returning fire. She wanted this to be up close and personal. She held her ground until the firing ceased. They took out charged batons and assaulted her. Nia avoided contact with the weapons, knowing that striking them with her sword would send a jolt that would slow her, if not render her unconscious. She spun low, cutting two attackers behind the knees. They fell, dropping their batons. A stick struck her back and she winced, stumbling toward another attacker waiting to catch her. Bad move. Nia drove her sword through them as she fell forward. They struck the ground, Nia on top. She rolled onto her back and kicked the baton wielder in the groin. As he doubled over, she grabbed his collar and slammed his face into the street, using the momentum to spring her back to feet. One assailant remained.

"You really want to do this?" Nia asked.

The assailant attacked. Nia waited until the last second then sidestepped as she slashed the woman across the abdomen. The woman fell onto her innards.

Nia strode toward the main street as people emerged from hiding to look at the grim remains of her work.

"Ship, what's Coco's status?"

"She is in negotiations. They do not seem to be going well."

"Coordinates."

Coco's position popped in her stream. Nia sprinted through the streets arriving at the Teatha government building ten minutes later. The door was unguarded, which was a mistake. Workers made way for Nia, their eyes swinging from her face to her sword. When she burst into council chambers, Coco was sitting in her seat, her dogs neutered by building security. Mayor Mornico turned to look at her, a smug smile on his rugged bearded face.

"Miss Nia!" he said. "Glad you could join us. Now I won't have to repeat myself."

Nia smirked. The bastard must have shield protection to talk to her like that. She stopped a few meters from the mayor, then looked at Coco.

"How you feeling?" she asked.

"I've been better," Coco replied.

"We'll be done in a minute," Nia said.

"It's gonna take longer than that, pretty lady," Mornico said.

"Ship, disable building security," Nia said.

The power blinked.

"Disabled," Ship replied.

Mornico looked shocked the moment before Nia cut off his head. She turned her attention to the city council members sitting behind the dead mayor, his blood and oil splattered on their clothes.

"Listen up. I don't give a dog's dick which one of you takes this asshole's place. Whoever does will stay out of our business. Understand?"

The councilpersons that were still conscious nodded. Nia turned to Coco and extended her hand.

"Come on sugar. Let's go."

Coco stood and took her hand. The dogs activated, following them out of the room.

"You were right," Coco said. "I'm not built for this."

Nia smiled.

"No worries. You just take care of home base. Let me and Ship handle the rest."

Ship waited as they exited the building. Nia let go of Coco's hand then kissed her.

"When are you returning?" Coco asked.

"When I'm done," Nia replied.

She sauntered to the boarding ramp.

"I'll keep a scan out for you," Coco called out.

"You do that," Nia replied.

Nia made her way to control.

"Get us out of here," she said.

Ship initiated launch sequence then they rose slowly over the city.

"You know she won't keep her word," Ship said.

"I know," Nia replied. "As long as she stays out of my way, she'll be safe."

"And if she doesn't?"

Nia shrugged. "Then it was fun while it lasted."

"Where to?" Ship asked.

"Junkspace," Nia replied. "I need time to rest. And think."

"And after that?" Ship asked.

Nia grinned. "Who knows?"

Cane

The merchant ship Chrysalis sat low on the ocean waves; her cargo hold packed with the fruits of a generous Mythrian harvest. Thaddus Lean, her owner and captain, did not usually trade for grain; it was perishable and yielded scant profit. But the Winds conspired this Cycle and created a once in a lifetime opportunity he couldn't pass up. While the Mythrian farmers complained of low prices because of the bounty, the hapless folk of Gebrel suffered from their third year of drought, their fields barren. The mountainous nation had wealthy gold reserves, but what use is gold when there's nothing to eat? With a pound of grain trading for the equivalent of a pound of precious metal, Thaddus Lean was about to become the richest merchant among the Spires.

He was about to let loose a laugh when the voice caught his ear. A chill ran from his cheek to his spine. For a moment he considered ignoring it. It was probably a seabird in the distance, a stray gray-will pushed too far from the shore by callous winds. But then he heard the lyrics, the soft sweet words drifting on the gentle sea like a lover's call.

Gray waves swell on a churning sea,
Firelight dancing like a joyful sprite,
Ships burn bright for all to see,
Sailors' souls rise into the night.

"Siren," he whispered.

"Siren!" a sailor shouted from the crow's nest.

The deck exploded into activity without one word from Thaddus. Any sailor worth their money belt knew what that song meant, even if he did not understand the language. Mercenary musketeers scaled the masts then took their perches. Cannon ports opened and the guns rolled into the position. The Chrysalis was a merchant vessel, which meant they would be outgunned. But they were prepared. Thaddus was not going to lose his fortune without a fight.

The ship waited in silent tension as the Siren's schooner approached. It was a small ship but armed to the teeth with cannon and pirates. The masts bristled with musketeers and the deck seethed with armed boarders. As it sailed closer, Thaddus saw her, sitting like a princess on an evening jaunt, her beautiful sepia face angled toward the sky as she crooned. Despite the desperate situation he found himself entranced, listening to her voice as she sang a song of love and loss.

The spell was broken by the call of his name.

"Thaddus Lean!"

Thaddus blinked. Siren no longer gazed into the heavens. Her caramel eyes were locked on him.

"I'm sure you think we have come to steal your cargo," she shouted. "But that is not so. We have come to buy it."

Thaddus's first mate, Kelan Gould, appeared at his side. The tall bronze man was also the senior guildsman and had a personal stake in the cargo.

"Don't listen to that wench!" he said. "She's here to steal it and end us!"

Thaddus looked at the man as if he was a giraffe.

"You expect us to fight when she's willing to pay?"

"Of course!" Kellan replied. "She's lying!"

Thaddus sucked his teeth.

"What's your offer, Siren?"

"Twenty gold crowns," she replied.

It was far less than Thaddus would receive if he delivered the cargo, but much more than he would have received under normal circumstances. Add his life to the deal and it was well worth it.

"We refused," Kelan shouted before Thaddus could reply. "I am Kelan Gould of the Gebrelan Shippers Guild. Twenty gold crowns is an insult. We can get three times as much in Gebrel. Make a better offer sea bitch or get out of our way."

Siren's smile faded.

"Thaddus, does this fool speak for you?"

"No," Thaddus responded quickly.

Siren's smile returned.

"Kelan Gould of the Gebrel Shippers Guild, apparently you have mistaken this as a negotiation. Brak!"

A musket barked and Kelan jerked then fell dead to the deck, a lead ball in his forehead. Thaddus looked up to see a burly bare-chested man in Siren's crow's nest lowering his flintlock to reload.

The ships were close enough for boarding. Siren and a dozen pirates swung over on ropes. Thaddus's crew stood armed, but even he knew they were no match for Siren's battle-hardened sea dogs. Siren sauntered to Thaddus then took a leather pouch from her waist belt.

"Half your payment. You'll get the rest when we reach port."

"Which port?" Thaddus asked.

"Don't worry about that," Siren replied. "My sailors will take the helm. Go to your cabin and rest, Thaddus. There's nothing for you to do here."

Siren was walking away when Thaddus called out.

"Why pay me? You could have taken it all."

Siren faced him and smiled. "Fighting would have damaged the cargo. I need it intact."

Thaddus watched her as she gave orders to her crew. He gazed at Kelan's body and realized it could have been him. He would take Siren's advice. There was a bottle of rum in his cabin that needed his attention.

* * *

Siren watched Thaddus until he disappeared below deck then set about securing his ship. She had waited months for him. Her plan would fail without his cargo. Now that it was secure she could begin the next phase of her plan. She had a good, brave, and hardworking crew but she needed more. She was not the trustful sort, but circumstances drove her to push the limits on her ways. There was no better time than now, and time was of the essence.

It took three weeks to sail to Bracken's Cove, one week longer than she anticipated. No person rules the sea, the saying went, a quote proven true during their journey. But she would not dwell on what she could not change. It was time to work on the second part of her plan.

Malik, her blood brother, sauntered up to her. He was shirtless as always, his pantaloons gathered around his waist with his wide belt. He wore his sword, which was rare. He hugged her waist and she smiled.

"You're wearing your sword," she said. "You never liked the Cove."

"It's not that I don't like it. I don't trust it. Too many of us here."

"They are not us," Siren said. "Remember that."

Malik laughed. "We've been at this for ten years. I think it's safe to say that we are the same as them."

Siren gripped the bulwark, her arms trembling. "We will never be the same as them."

"So, you're mad at me?" Malik asked.

"I don't want to be," she replied. "Everything we've done has been according to plan, even coming here."

"For a moment I thought you'd forgotten."

In truth, she had. So many years wasted running away from a promise. But they were not all wasted. She was a captain now with a reputation that resonated far beyond her territory.

"I'm back now," she answered. "I could never forget the people we left in the cane."

The ships eased into the docks nearest the tavern district. She was there to meet a man, one that would support her plan for his own reasons. Siren went below to Thaddus's cabin. She knocked and the merchant cracked open the door.

"Come with me," she said.

"You're finally going to kill me?" he asked. He was too drunk to be afraid.

"Don't be in such a hurry to die. I need your presence."

"I knew you would succumb to my charms," Thaddus slurred.

Siren laughed. "I heard you were a humorous sort."

Siren led Thaddus back on deck.

"Brak! Knife! Malik!" she shouted. "Come with me. The rest of you stay with the ships. We dock for one night only. Tomorrow, we sail."

She ignored the groans of her crew as she and the others disembarked then made their way to *The*

Cradle. The streets teemed with people, most drunk and the rest lurking with serious intent. She hated the Cove as much as Malik, but these types of hovels had been their life ever since they escaped the cane fields. Anything was better than the cane. Anything was better than slavery.

The Cradle's entrance was filthy and crowded as always.

"Brak, stay here and keep a lookout," Siren ordered.

The hulking man nodded then positioned himself beside the dilapidated door. Their group caught the attention of The Cradle's patrons as they entered. Siren received more than a few leers and lewd comments as they made their way to an empty table near the center of the crowded tavern. A thin man in a flowing shirt, leather pantaloons and dingy apron follow them.

"Welcome back, Siren," the man sang as they sat.

"Barron," Siren said. "You're still alive, I see."

Barron Stiffwind, owner of The Cradle, smiled, revealing his unnaturally perfect teeth.

"This place hasn't killed me yet."

"Keep your pistols loaded," Malik said.

"And your knife sharp," Knife said.

"Truth," Barron replied. He cut a mean glance at Thaddus.

"So, you're hanging out with merchants now?"

"For the moment," Siren replied. "I could use some of that swill you call coffee."

Barron laughed then waddled away, returning moments later with a steaming cup. He sat it down and was about to add sugar before he stopped.

"I almost forgot," he said, a hint of fear in his voice. "Forgive me, Siren."

Siren grinned. "No worries. It's been a long time."

"I'd like some," Thaddus said.

Barron's eyes narrowed. "No, you wouldn't."

He took the sugar then shuffled away. Thaddus scowled.

"So, you don't like sugar?" he asked.

Siren sipped her coffee. "It tastes like blood. Our blood."

Thaddus's eyebrows rose. "I'm sorry. How insensitive of me."

"Ha! There she is!"

The lean stranger pushed his way through the patrons to their table then sat before Siren. Knife and Malik rose from their seats, but she waved them down.

"Who are you and what do you want?"

"I want to sail with you," he said. "Name's Mattew Jan."

"I don't need more crew," Siren said. "Be off with you."

"I spent six years on the Griff under Captain Braddock," Mattew said. "They don't come any tougher that him, or me."

Mattew smirked then leaned back in his chair and folded his tattooed arms across his chest.

"You ever work the cane?" Siren asked.

"Yes!" he replied.

"Brak!"

Brak entered the tavern, pushing people and tables aside as he made his way to Siren and the others. Mattew's eyes swelled, and his mouth hung open as the hulking black skinned man arrived.

"I'll leave you be," Mattew said as he stood to leave. Siren unsheathed her machete then laid it on the table.

"You'll stay where you are."

Brak stood beside her, his sword scars heaving with his chest. He stared unblinking at Mattew.

"Brak, this man says he worked the cane," Siren said.

Brak laughed hard and loud for at least a minute. He grabbed Mattew from his seat then slammed him face first onto the table with his right hand. With his left hand he ripped off the man's shirt. Siren stood then looked at the man's back.

"I thought so," she said.

She turned her back to everyone then lifted her shirt. Ragged keloid scars marred her dark skin. Brak grabbed Mattew's hair, pulling his head back so he could see the gruesome sight.

"This is what the cane does to you," Siren said. "There's nothing harder than the cane."

She dropped her shirt then sat back in her seat.

"You can go now Brak," Siren said.

Brak shoved Mattew's face into the table before he walked away. Mattew's nose bled as he lifted his head.

"Every person on my ship has worked the cane," she said. "Hell is a relief to us. Heaven is a place we'll never see."

She lifted her machete then pointed it at Mattew.

"Now I ask you again. Have you worked the cane?"

"No," Mattew confessed. "I'm . . . I'm sorry. I'll leave you be."

Siren's movement was swifter than the eye. She cut off the tip of Mattew's little finger then pressed the machete's edge against his throat before he could cry out. She leaned close to his ear.

"A warning," she whispered.

Mattew fell from his chair and ran out of The Cradle, holding his wounded hand. Siren settled into her chair and sipped her coffee, ignoring Thaddus's stare.

"He lied to me," she said, answering his unspoken question.

Brak entered the tavern again. He was not alone. A man with skin like darkness followed him, as tall as the brooding giant but not as broad. His leather breeches were like a second skin over his muscled legs, his leather jerkin tight against his chest. A cutlass and a dozen jeweled daggers hung from his wide waist belt. He smiled at Siren, exposing his teeth, the lower molars capped with gold. Siren returned his smile.

The man turned the empty chair backwards then straddle the seat and rested his folded arms on the backrest.

"Jonas. You came," Siren said.

"I would never refuse you, queen," Jonas replied. He took a dagger from his belt then placed it on the table. The blade was pure silver fitted into a hilt of carved ivory speckled with rubies and emeralds.

"I had this made for you in Carmalin," he said.

Siren reached for the knife, brushing Jonas's hand as she picked it up. She admired the craftsmanship.

"It's beautiful," she said. "Not very practical, but exquisite."

Jonas beamed. "Not nearly as beautiful as you."

Malik rolled his eyes and sucked his teeth. Jonas looked his way and his smile faded.

"Malik, how are you? I didn't notice you."

"You never do." Malik stood. "I'll take my leave. Thaddus, come with me. These two have 'business' to discuss."

Malik leaned close to her.

"I still don't trust him. You know what he wants."
Siren gazed into Jonas's hazel eyes.

"Of course I do," she said to Malik. "But he won't
get it here. I'll be fine."

Malik gave Jonas another nasty look before taking Thaddus to another table.

"That one fancies you," Jonas said. Siren waved
her hand dismissively.

"Malik is my brother," she replied. "By bond if
not by blood. We look out for each other. You are
the one who fancies me."

"As do half the corsairs that sail the True Sea," he
said.

"And yet none of them came with you, did they?"

Jonas frowned. "No, they didn't. Most would give
up half their treasures to bed you but not their
lives."

"I'm not a whore," Siren said, her voice tinged
with anger. She slammed her fist on the table.

Jonas raised his hands. "I never meant to imply
that, queen. There is no person the Black Brother-
hood respects more."

"Then why are they not here?"

"Let's be practical," Jonas said. "What you plan
yields no booty. Besides, the Dalmatin Coast is
treacherous, especially this time of year."

"I know that coast well," she said. "I know every
bay, inlet, and harbor. I could sail it with my eyes
shut."

"You can, but we can't," Jonas replied. "Which
leaves you with me."

"And why are you here alone?" she asked, even
though she knew the answer.

"I came to give you the dagger," he said, grin-
ning.

"We sail in the morning," she said.

"I'll be ready," Jonas replied.

Jonas stood then took a deep bow before striding from the tavern. Malik and Thaddus returned to the table.

"How many will come?" Malik asked.

"Only Jonas."

"Then we must end it."

"No," Siren said. "The conditions are perfect. It may be years before they're like this again. It's now or never." She heard her voice crack when she said the words. She knew Malik heard it too.

"We can't do it with only two ships," Malik insisted. "We'll have to make arrangements for the others."

"And we will," Siren said. "Come, we have work to do."

The two of them stood to leave the tavern.

"What about me?" Thaddus asked.

"Enjoy the rest of the night," Siren said. "Tomorrow, we go to war."

* * *

Black sails crested the horizon, hidden from the shoreline watchtowers by dense fog. Though the harbor guards could not see the approaching vessels, Siren knew the shore well. It had once been her home, if a plantation could be considered such a thing.

She turned to Brak, standing shirtless beside her.

"Let's get to the boats," she said.

Together they marched to the bulwark and joined the others. These were the elite of her crew, men and women who had proven themselves time and time again in battle.

"We won't have much time," she said. "So stay diligent. They won't know we're coming so do the best you can to get them out. And remember, we only have so much space. Bring back only those you need."

Everyone nodded. She searched the deck before spotting Malik.

"Malik!" she shouted.

The lithe man hurried to her side.

"Are the cannons ready?"

"Yes, Siren," he said.

She glanced over his shoulder, the Kraken, Jonas's heavy ship, kept time with them. She could barely see him, but she knew he was there. Her attention returned to Malik. She raised her right arm as he did, the two of them setting the wrist clocks attached to their leather gloves.

"Begin the bombardment in ten minutes," Siren said. "We should be ashore by then."

"Yes, Siren," he said.

They touched their foreheads and shared a smile. Malik was her oldest and dearest friend. There was no one she trusted more.

"Bring them back, Akini," he said, using her little name.

"I will, Ajamu," she said.

They touched each other's cheek then broke away with their duties. When she faced her landing crew her smile was gone. She climbed over the bulwark then sat in the first boat hanging over the side. The others boarded and the boats were lowered into the choppy sea. Conditions were bad for a boat landing but perfect for her plan. They rowed to shore with eight boats; three carrying the landing party, three empty and two filled with supplies.

Ajamu's timing was perfect. The cannons roared as the boats ran aground. Siren leapt over the sides with the others, drawing her sword and pistol.

"Get the rifles and follow me," she ordered.

In moments they ran across the misty field, her memory unflagging. The cane appeared abruptly, and old memories of pain and drudgery hit her like a physical blow. She remembered her thin arms as a child clutching the cane stalks, the leaves cutting her skin like razors. The brutal work from sunup to sundown, then trying to stay awake as mama soothed her wounds with butter and kisses. The horror of finding dead workers among the stalks, souls worked to oblivion. She stumbled; Brak caught her before she fell.

"Are you alright, Siren?" he asked.

"Yes," she replied. She pulled away from his grasp, angry at her weakness.

They met the first overseer halfway through the fields. He turned on them, his eyes wide when he recognized what was happening. Siren drove her machete through his throat before he had time to shout. The second overseer stood by the slave shacks, too far to kill silently.

"Brak," she said.

Brak raised his musket and fired. The man's head jerked then he crumpled to the ground. Moments later the alarm drums rumbled.

Siren and the others quickened their pace. The other overseers appeared with muskets, swords and maces. They were no match for Siren and her corsairs. Siren shot her pistols empty then used them as clubs as he waded through the inept guards.

"Find your loved ones!" she shouted. "Time is short!"

She ran directly to the hut where her family lived. She burst inside and was greeted by their fearful faces.

"It's me," she said. "Don't you recognize me?"

Their terror transformed into joy.

"Akini!" they shouted.

The young ones enveloped her with hugs and tears. Mama was the last to come to her.

"You said you would come back," she said.

"And I did. Now come. We don't have much time."

"I can't run so fast," mama said. She opened her ragged cloak, revealing a swollen belly.

Siren's entire body burned with rage. "Is it his? Did he do this to you?"

Mama didn't reply.

She grabbed her mama's hand and pulled her from the hut. The others followed. The other families fled to the boats, bypassing those who did not have anyone to rescue them. A group of corsairs stood in the center of the village with the wrapped bundles Thaddus's cargo had bought.

"Take them to the boats," she told her mama. "They will take you to my ship."

"Where are you going?" mama asked.

"To help the others."

Siren kissed mama's cheek then joined her corsairs and the gathering workers.

"Listen to me!" she shouted. "I wish we could take you all with us, but we can't. We don't have enough ships. But I will not leave you defenseless. we will not leave you without a chance to free yourselves."

The men opened the bundles. There were muskets, pistols, swords, machetes, knives and bags of gunpower and musket balls.

"You can die in the fields, or you can fight for your freedom. Those who wish to escape should head toward the sunset. There is a city on the coast that will take you in without question. Your life won't be easy, but it will be better than this. May the Goddess protect you!"

The workers surged toward the weapons as Siren and the others hurried to the boats. Siren stood guard with Brak and Knife while the others clambered into the boats. Once everyone was loaded and on their way, Siren turned and strode back toward the plantation.

"Siren!" Brak called out. "Where are you going?"

Siren did not answer. She loaded her pistols then picked up and loaded a musket which lay beside one of the dead overseers. She found a horse, climbed on it then kicked the beast into a full gallop down the road leading to the grand house. The horse sprinted between fields of unharvested cane, much of it blazing from the relentless barrage of her ships. The cane faded, replaced by vegetable fields. The master's house loomed before her, and her anger flamed. As she neared the front gate, she spied militiamen running toward her. Siren pulled the first pistol from her baldric then pressed her body against the horse's neck. She slowed the animal to a trot as the militiamen neared. The first to reach her neared grabbed the horse's reins then glared at her.

"What's going on down there, wench?" he asked. "Is it pirates?"

Siren jerked upright, a pistol in each hand.

"Yes!"

She shot the militiaman in the forehead and the one behind him in the chest. Siren rolled off the horse and onto her feet, using the horse as a shield for her right flank as she confronted two militiamen advancing on her left. Both went down, musket balls in their faces. When more militiamen rounded the horse, Siren held her last loaded pistols. She dropped to her knees and took aim, shooting both men in the loins. She dropped her pistols and took theirs.

Siren was climbing onto the horse when a musket fired from a distance. A ball slammed into her shoulder, knocking her off her mount. Light flashed inside her head as she struck the mud. An image appeared; she was a girl surrounded by the opulence of the master's banquet room, singing for his guests. She looked at him and he stared back, his expression terrifying her. It was that day she decided to escape. She was already his work tool. She would not be his pleasure tool as well.

Siren shook her head clear. She struggled to her feet then climbed back onto her horse, wincing with pain. The distant musket fired again; this time the shooter missed. Siren spied him on the porch of the grand house. She took her musket from the saddle straps, using the horse's neck to steady her aim. The horse jumped when she fired, the musket smoke blinding her. When it cleared, she saw the marksman sprawled on the porch.

No one challenged her as she rode through the gates and up to the stairs leading into the mansion. Pistol in her right hand and sword in her left, she shoved the door open then entered. She instinctively dodged to the left, avoiding the ambush she knew awaited her. The foyer rang with the pistol's report; Siren waited for the smoke to clear before shooting a militiaman point blank in the face. She raised her machete, blocking the downward slash of another militiaman's sword before plunging her dagger into his gut. She spun away as the man fell to face the only person remaining in the room.

Graeme Kell, her former master, stood before her armed with a sword and dagger, a malicious smile on his face.

"Siren," he said. "So, you are the cause of this."

They circled each other, Siren's face twisted with hate.

"You have grown into a beautiful woman as I expected," he said. "You would have made an excellent concubine."

She screamed as she attacked. Graeme was skilled, but not as skilled as Siren. His smile faded with each cut inflicted; soon his eyes were wide with desperation ad he fought off her assault. Siren ignored every wound, her mind filled with one purpose. Her sword finally found its target, plunging into Graeme's torso just below his ribcage. Siren twisted her machete then ripped it out of him, creating a wound that couldn't' be healed.

Graeme tumbled to the floor. Siren stood over him, waiting until she knew there was no life left in him. She spat on his blank face.

She turned away, stumbling to the door as the toll of her wounds overtook her. She was about to collapse when two strong hands caught her. She looked up into Brak's stoic face.

"We must go," he said. "More militiamen are coming.

She leaned against Brak as they ran to her horse. He helped her mount then together they rode to a waiting boat. Brak took the oars and rowed into the waters. Siren lay on her back facing the burning plantation until exhaustion pulled her into darkness.

* * *

Siren, Malik, Brak, and Jonas climbed the steep slope, their clothes sticking to their skin, their chests heaving with exertion. Siren reached the hill summit first then sat hard in the knee-high grass, letting out a relieved sigh. She took her water gourd from her waist belt and took a long swig. By the time she lowered it the others sat beside her in various states of exhaustion.

'Was this necessary?" Jonas asked.

"You said you wanted to see the island," Siren replied. "This is the best place to do it."

She stood then pulled Jonas to his feet. Her shoulder still ached from the wound she received at the plantation, the musket ball still inside. Once everything settled, she would have a healer remove it. They stood side by side, the entire expanse of the island visible.

"I'm impressed," Jonas said. "Very impressed. How did you find it?"

"I studied the maps of Old Zimbabawa,' Siren replied. "I searched for an island far from the main trade routes, somewhere we could be hidden from the rest of the world, and a place easy to defend. This island was considered a legend even in the old days. We are not the first to live here."

She pointed due west. "There are ruins there. The people who once lived here were great builders."

She pointed north. "That's where we'll settle. The land is good and it's far enough from the coast so not to be spotted by any passing ships. We'll build a fort on this summit as a lookout for interlopers and set up a signal system to warn us."

She then pointed east. "That's where we'll grow the cane. The conditions are perfect for it."

Jonas looked surprised. "Grow cane? I thought that would be the last thing you would do."

"Some of us still have a liking for it," Siren replied. "It will also be a reminder of what we endured and what will never happen again."

"I see," Jonas said. "And what will you call this little paradise?"

"Sirenity," Malik said.

"No," Siren replied.

"It is a good name," Brak said.

"I don't agree," Siren replied.

"I like it too," Jonas said.

The three of them stared at her. Siren smirked.

"It's a possibility," she finally said. "But the people will decide."

They began their descent. Malik and Brak walked ahead while Jonas and Siren walked together.

"So, is there a place in your world for a wandering corsair?" Jonas asked.

Siren cut her eyes at him.

"That's up to the corsair. But don't expect to be asked. I have no intentions of becoming anyone's wife anytime soon."

Jonas frowned. "After all I've done for you?"

Siren sucked her teeth. "After all you've done for yourself. You were paid, quite well I might add."

Jonas laughed. "True. I suspect you'll marry one day and have a dozen children."

"I wouldn't wait on that day," Siren replied. "My days on the sea are not done."

Jonas's eyebrows rose. "Really?"

"There were so many we couldn't rescue," Siren said. "I plan to find them all and bring them here."

"Then I will help you," Jonas said.

Siren grinned. "There will be no pay in this, corsair."

"Consider it an investment," Jonas replied.

Siren smiled. "So be it."

They reached the base of the summit then followed the trail back to the village. Siren was about to catch up with Brak and Malik when Jonas grabbed her arm.

"One more thing. What is your real name?"

Siren didn't' reply.

"Please, you must tell me!" he pleaded. "I can't stand Malik knowing something about you that I don't. You owe me that much."

Siren laughed. "Akini. My name is Akini."

"Akini," Jonas repeated. "A lovely name, but I prefer Siren. It describes you perfectly. Lovely yet deadly."

Siren rolled her eyes. "Whatever, corsair. Come, we can discuss our plans as we walk."

"As you command, Akini of Sirenity!"

Jonas took a deep bow and Siren laughed. For the first time she could remember, there was real joy in her heart. She would make sure it remained.

End

Milton Davis is an award winning Black Speculative fiction writer and owner of MVmedia, LLC, a publishing company specializing in Science Fiction and Fantasy based on African/African Diaspora history, culture and traditions. Milton is the author of thirty novels and short story collections. Milton is also a contributing author to Black Panther: Tales of Wakanda, published by Marvel and Titan Books *and coauthor of Hadithi and the State of Black Speculative Fiction* with Eugen Bacon. He is the editor and co-editor of eleven anthologies, most recently Cyberfunk! published by MVmedia, LLC. Milton's story 'The Swarm' was nominated for the 2017 British Science Fiction Association Award for Short Fiction and his story, Carnival, was nominated for the 2020 British Science Fiction Association Award for Short Fiction. Milton is a 2022 recipient of the East Coast Black Age of Comics Convention Lifetime Pioneer Achievement Award. Visit his website, www.miltonjdavis.com for more information.

For more books by Milton J. Davis and other exciting MVmedia titles, visit our website.
www.mvmediaatl.com

9 798985 733686